Becoming Us

BECOMING US

BECCA SEYMOUR

For all of the step parents in the world. Thank you for choosing to love your children as your own.

CHAPTER ONE

A QUIET GROAN ESCAPED THE MAN AT MY SIDE. THE sound had me grinning. "Morning," I whispered. While the alarm had gone off, I didn't want to break the morning haze.

"Umm-mmm."

Not sure if Scott was giving a strangled, garbled message, purring, or simply not fully awake, I turned over to face him. His eyes were closed, but a soft smile splayed his lips.

I pressed my own to his mouth, gave him a quick peck, and pulled back. "You awake?" Humor lightened my words.

Scott was not a morning person. For the past six months of us living together, I'd quickly discovered that caffeine and a pastry, or even better, pancakes and bacon, made morning Scott a much nicer guy to be around.

And I had zero problem with that.

Just like I managed his morning woes, he not only wrangled my manic three-year-old, he also clamped his mouth shut when I dumped my dirty clothes on the floor just a few feet away from the laundry basket.

I knew it was a dick move, but after a long day at the coffee shop, spending exhausting, fun hours with Libby, and catching up with everything else that needed doing, that damn basket became my Achilles.

"Was that really the alarm?" He forced one eye open before closing it again.

I snorted. "Afraid so. You can stay in bed, but I have to get my ass up and ready. Jasper's opening for me, but I need to get on top of the weekend prep."

Business was good. While there'd been a turnover in staff due to college starting up, some moving away and such, the past eight months had been solid. Jenna, Scott's sister, was still with me full-time. It took a heap of stress and worry off my shoulders, having someone I trusted implicitly.

We managed to balance shifts fairly, so we were able to work just one weekend each a month as well as managing to be available for our kids.

Though having Scott, and sometimes Carter or Tanner, sorting the pickups and drop-offs too helped. Tanner and I had previously made a good team, but now, with Scott by my side and the addition of Jenna and her boys, we'd become a big extended family.

It worked.

Scott nodded, face still burrowed in the pillow. "I can happily stay in bed."

I pulled myself away from the warm sheets, the chill of the floorboards making me shiver. The holidays were fast approaching, and the weather seemed to be keeping up nicely. We hadn't had snow, but it was colder than a witch's tit some nights.

Once showered and dressed, I returned to our bedroom and leaned over Scott once more, my knee to the bed. He rolled into me and angled his face, knowing what I wanted.

"Love you," I said just as I kissed him. I made to pull away, but his hand clamped on the back of my head, and his mouth opened a little. His tongue swept against the seam of my lips, and I parted for him. I swore, every time this man laid one on me, I became putty in his hands.

The kiss slowed, and I lifted away. My eyes

searched his deep brown ones before roaming to his lips. "I wish I could stay."

Scott no longer looked as sleepy. Instead, heat swirled in his gaze. "I know. Later, your ass is mine." His hand brushed across my thigh and landed on one of my butt cheeks. He gave a light squeeze. "Love you. Have a good day."

"You too." One more brief kiss and I was able to tear myself away.

I crept past Libby's room, not wanting to wake her. Last night she'd woken a couple of times grumbling about something. Her temperature was okay, so whatever had made her wake, I hoped it wouldn't happen again.

Not bothering with a coffee since I'd grab one at work, I headed out. Before I knew it, I was in the kitchen, elbow-deep in pastry and bobbing my head to a dodgy beat Jasper had put on.

"Dare I ask what this song is called?" I asked when Jasper stepped into the kitchen to grab stock for the front counter.

He threw me a mischievous grin. "Too trendy and upbeat for you, old man?" He ducked when I threw a small ball of pastry at him.

"I'm not that damn old," I grumbled. "Just 'cause you're wet behind the ears and have hearing you're still yet to destroy doesn't mean I'm not down with the kids."

I winced, and he laughed. Yeah, saying such bullshit meant I was getting past it. What the hell? I was barely in my midthirties, but since being a dad, and especially after too many sleepless nights, I felt a hell of a lot more ancient than that.

"You want me to ignore that?" Jasper asked, picking up the pastry I'd thrown and dumping it in the trash.

"Yeah, that'd be best."

"You and Scott should come to the city one weekend with me. I'm heading out in a couple of weekends, meeting some friends and hitting a club."

The look on my face made him snort, so I followed with "Maybe. I'll ask Scott."

"Ha! That means no, right?"

"No." *Yes.* "It just means I'll ask Scott." The thought of heading out for a night of drinks and dancing wasn't what put me off. Hell, getting my buzz on and grinding against Scott was almost enough to get me saying hell yes, but the potential hangover if I drank too much, let alone the late night, had me internally moaning at the thought.

Yes, I was seriously past it.

"I'm staying in a motel just a couple of miles from

the club. It's cheap and cheerful. It'll mean the Uber's cheap too."

I smiled at Jasper, thinking about our differences. He was twenty-three, a college grad who'd returned to town to support his mom after his dad's passing, and a genuinely nice kid. He was also so overqualified for the position that I kinda felt guilty he was still working for me and letting his teaching degree go to waste. The problem with such a small town as Kirkby was with only one high school close by and the next a good sixty miles away, it made teaching positions really difficult to get.

It also meant the poor guy was dealing with the wages from the coffeeshop alone. Yeah, I paid above minimum wage, but it wasn't that much in the grand scheme of things.

"Honestly, I'll think about it and chat to Scott." Admittedly, it had been a while since Scott and I had some alone time. Not that it was a hardship to spend our time with Libby and at home.

I grinned internally, still crazy happy that Scott had agreed to move in with me. It had all worked out. Especially since Jenna was able to take over his place.

"Sure thing," Jasper answered as he headed back out to finish setting up.

The day whizzed on by after that. Between the weekend prep, doing some paperwork, and saying hi to Carter, who stopped by on his lunch break, I considered more and more that a night out of town just may be a good thing.

When Scott came by, Libby holding his hand, I pulled them both into a hug and planted a kiss on both their cheeks. "Hey, you two. That time already?" I glanced at my watch, realizing I was due to wrap up and head on home.

"It sure is." Scott offered that sexy-as-hell smile he reserved solely for me. My gut tightened with the memory of this morning's kiss. The thought of a night away with zero interruptions so we could turn it into one of debauchery was looking even better when heat crept up his neck.

I rarely held back how much Scott affected me and meant to me. And after a couple of years together, all it took was a glance for him to know exactly what was on my mind.

Pulling my gaze away from Scott, I focused on Libby and crouched before her. "You had a great day?"

She nodded enthusiastically and almost socked me in the eye as she thrust out her arm to show me what she was wearing. "Made it with my Scott." A quick glance in Scott's direction showed me he melted at her words. It got the both of us every time.

"Wow. Pretty bracelet there, princess. You two did a great job."

"Yep." She looked thoroughly proud of herself. "And I made you one." She turned her gaze up to Scott. "Daddy's?"

"I've got it right here." Scott grinned down at her and pulled out a bright pink and green beaded bangle, with the odd bead having tinsel and some glitter attached. "I told you Daddy would love it. Here you go." He handed it over, a shit-eating grin on his face.

I had zero doubt my fixed smile was more of a grimace, but there was pretty much nothing I wouldn't do for my girl. She was spoiled rotten, and I had zero regrets about that. Plus, I'd wear whatever crazy stuff she created with absolute pride.

Just last week she'd discovered makeup, courtesy of Jenna. I'd managed to snap a photo of Scott complete with blue and green eyeshadow, something red and slimy on his cheeks with glitter on it, an orange lipstick that had made my sides hurt from laughing so much, and a black crayon or pen or something drawn all around his eyes.

While the same had been done to me, it was

Scott's hairclips and butterflies that had set his image off spectacularly.

We were both suckers.

We also had to pay Jenna back somehow for the makeup kit she'd provided.

With the elastic bracelet snapped into place on my wrist, I jiggled it.

"It's soooo pwety." Her pretty eyes were opened wide. "My Scott has one. Look, Daddy." She tugged at Scott's arm so he knelt, then snapped the grotesque necklace on his neck. Scott winced.

"Careful there, Libby. Don't destroy Scott's windpipe." I grinned widely at Scott, who, complete with bright and dodgy-looking necklace, was freakin' gorgeous. How could he not be when he wore the love he had for Libby so openly?

"Sorry." She spun to face Scott and threw her arms around his neck. After a big squeeze, she planted a loud kiss on his mouth. "You 'kay?"

Scott stood with her in his arm. "I sure am. I think this pretty necklace has magical powers, or maybe it's your kiss."

I stood and looked on as Libby nodded.

"I fink it's my kisses."

"Makes sense," he said.

After another bob of her head, she gave him one

more kiss. "Love you." She then wriggled her whole body to get down.

Scott's smile lit up his face. "Love you too, Libby." He set her on her feet, and she raced off to Jessie, one of my staff, who was clearing tables. His gaze on me, he asked, "You almost done?"

"Give me five and I'm all yours."

His eyes turned molten, urging me to get my ass into gear and spend the rest of the afternoon and evening with my favorite two people.

CHAPTER TWO

SCOTT

SPENDING MY DAY OFF WITH LIBBY WAS AS exhausting as it was enjoyable. I loved every minute of spending time with her. Adored coloring, playing with her cars, brushing the hair on her My Little Ponies. None of that meant it wasn't hard work. Between chasing her around, trying to keep the house straight—which I gave up on after she spent an hour dressing up and showing me via the parade we'd set up—I had no doubt as soon as she was unconscious, I'd be following and collapsing into bed.

But now being at home, Davis by my side and Libby at the table drawing, peace thrummed through me.

I'd never been truly content until I'd moved in

with the two of them after not-too-much persuasion.

"You're on call this weekend, right?"

I peered over at Davis, who was preparing a salad to go with the lasagna heating in the oven I'd made earlier. "Yeah. From—" I glanced at the wall clock. "—now actually, till Monday morning." We didn't get that many after-hours callouts at the clinic, but there were usually one or two minor incidents that would take me away. While I had enough staff at my veterinary clinic to fill the on-call load, I'd made it a point when scheduling to balance the roster as fairly as possible. It meant we each only had to cover one weekend every five weeks. It made everyone happy.

It was one of the first changes I'd made when I'd finally stepped up to managing the place.

When Davis didn't respond right away, I glanced over at him. "What are you thinking?" I prompted.

"Do you want to head to the city in a couple of weekends, to a club?"

My eyes widened and interest sparked through me. "A club, as in music, dancing, and drinks?" It had been a couple of years since I'd been out of Kirkby, let alone clubbing. Then a thought hit me. "As in a gay club?" My gut clenched in interest.

Having come out not long before I met Davis, I'd

only ever experienced one gay bar. Every second I'd been in the joint I'd been terrified.

A club with Davis, though…. The idea sent a thrill of anticipation through me.

I'd come a long way since moving to Kin and befriending Carter and then falling for Davis. The chance to have a night out with him was something I could get on board with.

Davis shrugged. "I think so, but I'll check with Jasper."

"Jasper?"

"Yeah. He invited us to head out with him. Thought we could stay the night and book into a seedy motel. Maybe we could go old-school and find one with a vibrating bed or something." He waggled his brows at me, and I snorted.

Jasper seemed like a nice guy. I knew Davis liked him, so spending a night out was no hardship. "We don't need a vibrating bed for me to rock your world." I winked, my grin wide. I followed up with laughter and caught the tomato he threw at me, popping it in my mouth.

He rolled his eyes. "So what do you think?"

I nodded. "As long as my sister or Carter and Tanner are happy to have our girl, then I like the idea."

His gaz softened as he walked over to me. A quick kis on my lips was followed by his face pressing inst my neck and him inhaling.

Wra ng my arms around him, I squeezed tightly ot that I'm complaining, but any reason why e sniffing me?"

ngers found my side and he dug in, making m and pull away laughing.

m ybe. And you'll find out after Libby's e."

o bed yet," Libby said. We both turned in her ion. Her gaze intent, she looked ready for e.

Davis headed back to the kitchen as I stepped to by's side. "Not yet. Dinner, bath, story, then bed."

Under her scrutiny for a few more beats, I held ack my smirk. "Okay. Chocolate and fish for dinner?"

Davis made a gagging sound. "What the heck have you been feeding her when I've been at work?"

I sniggered and shook my head. "Lasagna, and then maybe chocolate ice cream afterward if you eat it all up."

Pencil in mouth, she looked seriously in thought. A swift nod followed, along with a "'Kay."

Wide-eyed, I looked at Davis and blew out my cheeks. He simply grinned and finished off the salad.

With dinner and bath time over, Davis read Libby a story while I read through my latest copy of *PetVet*. The three of us were snuggled in bed. It was one of my favorite times of the day. Quiet time for the three of us.

"And the troll wasn't quite sure which way was up and which way was down. But it didn't matter. As long as the sky was blue and the grass was green and he had his friends Fairy and Bunny by his side, he was the happiest troll in the world." Davis closed the book and looked over at me, crossing his eyes.

I gave a silent chuckle and clamped my lips together.

"Come on, princess. Wee and bed," Davis said after pressing a kiss to her fair head.

"My Scott, carry?" She cast her sleepy gaze to me.

My heart full, I silently stood and swept her in my arms, taking her to the bathroom.

A few short moments later, she was tucked up in bed and Davis and I were backing away after singing a goofy version of a *Little Mermaid* song.

"Coffee or something stronger?" Davis asked.

"Beer would be good."

"On it." He headed for the kitchen while I made it to the couch.

I relaxed into the cushions and sighed, which was quickly followed up by a yawn.

"You sure you don't just need to collapse into bed?" Davis passed me the bottle of beer.

I accepted it gratefully, took a sip rather than chugging it, and quirked my brow at him. "I'm not that bad." Though truth be told, I was sure both of us could pass out easily from our busy days. "Get your ass over here and tell me about your day."

He did so, angling toward me, one leg up and his knee pressing on my thigh. "Same old, really. Have you spoken to Jenna today?"

I shook my head. "Nope. Not since Wednesday."

He pressed his lips together, seeming to debate something.

"Spill it."

"She has a date tomorrow night."

With the bottle next to my mouth, I paused. Eyes wide, I took a moment to process. Removing my drink and settling it on my lap, I kept a tight grip as I responded, "With Mick?" I knew my sister had been chatting to him recently, and she'd admitted to me she liked him and was considering a date, but that was about a month ago. Truth be told, I hadn't thought about it much since.

"Yep." Davis smiled at me. "She was all gushy and shit when she told me. Nervous as heck too. I told her the boys could sleep here tomorrow night."

I nodded, though not quite sure about her house being empty.

"You will not camp out at her house," Davis said pointedly to me. He knew me so damn well.

A grin settled on my lips. "What? I'd never—"

"Bullshit. Your sister is a grown-ass woman, Mick's a good guy and knows better than to be a dick, and this'll be good for her."

He spoke the truth. Since her divorce was finalized last year, she'd been a heap happier and more settled, and Mick was the first guy she'd been interested in. They'd actually danced around each other for at least five months. It didn't mean I wouldn't be watching out for her, though. "You're right."

Davis grinned at that. "I usually am."

I snorted.

"You disagreeing with me?" He arched a brow. I loved it when he threw me that look. The "I'll make you beg until you agree with me" one. It worked every time at getting me worked up and hot and bothered.

"I wouldn't dream of it." I placed my bottle down on the coffee table. "But if I did—"

He all but launched himself at me. A laugh burst free just as his mouth connected with mine. It melted away quickly with the heat of the kiss, the brush of his tongue, and the movement of him positioning himself to straddle my thighs.

I angled his head away, and he peered down at me. When his eyes connected with mine, my heart hit my chest even harder. He was fucking beautiful all the time. But like this. Needy. Wanting my mouth. Wanting to connect. He was everything.

"Bed or here?" His breath washed over me with his husky words.

With my hand on his belt buckle, I answered, "Here works for me."

───

WE'D HAD ANOTHER ROUGH NIGHT WITH LIBBY. THIS time she had a temperature. By five, Davis and I gave up and got out of bed. Fresh coffee on the table before me, I inhaled, hoping it would help to clear the fog. A noise in the hallway alerted me to Davis returning.

"Coffee's here." I offered him a small smile as he entered the kitchen/diner. "She settled again?"

With a loud yawn, he stretched. His shorts sat low, and his tee rose high. I appreciated the sight but had zero energy to give the sliver of skin more than a happy thought. "Thanks." He sat next to me after pressing a kiss on my head. "Her temp's come down a little. I gave her another dose of Tylenol, and she's finally dozed off."

"That's good."

"Yeah. I'll see what she's like when she wakes, see if she's still grumbly and what her temp is like, and if I need to, I'll call the out-of-hours service at the clinic."

"Yeah. I've never seen her so unsettled before." I'd only missed out on the first ten months or so of Libby, and in that time was certain of several things where she was concerned. She was happy and smiley, with a cheeky-as-hell personality, especially when it came to playing tricks on Davis. Her speech was impressive, and she'd never had more than a couple of colds in the past couple of years. Yeah, she had moments of being pissed off for whatever reason—usually because we said no—but her tantrums were rare and didn't last long.

This time her behavior was different. She was clearly unwell, so a doctor's visit was a good call.

"I hate it when she feels like shit. I've asked her a few times where she hurts, but each time she tells me a different location." Davis sighed. He looked shattered. I'd only got up the once in the night, while he had three times.

"If you want to head back to bed, you can. I'm up and know I won't be able to go back to sleep again."

"You sure?"

I nodded. "Absolutely."

A relieved smile settled on his face. "Thanks." He stood, coffee mug in hand, and kissed me. "Prod me if you need me." Usually, the mention of a prod would become something salacious. Though his eyes twinkled a little and his mouth quirked, only sleep was in Davis's future.

"No problem. Ass to bed, now. I've got laundry to do and will listen out for Libby."

He brushed his fingers against my shoulder as he made to leave, and sipping my coffee, I watched him go, eyes on his butt.

Once alone, I yawned and shook my head.

There was no point procrastinating. Chores didn't get themselves done.

An hour and a half later, I heard Libby's door

open. Immediately I headed her way and scooped her up. Despite still being hot to touch, relief swept through me when she welcomed me with a smile.

"How are you feeling, baby girl?" I asked as I headed to the kitchen with her in my arms.

"'Kay." She rubbed at her eyes. Pink stained her cheeks, and her eyes were a little glazed.

"You still feeling ill?"

She gave me a pitiful nod and this time held on to her ear. "Hurts."

"Your ear?" I clarified.

She nodded before wriggling in my arms. "Cake pease."

I chuckled and set her on her feet. "Maybe after breakfast you can have a giant piece of cake, yeah?"

"Giant," she repeated, her eyes widening. "This big?" When she spread her arms wide, I laughed, tickling her tummy.

"I'll see what I can do." After grabbing her a cup of juice, I collected the thermometer. "Let's sit you up here." I picked Libby up to sit on a chair at the table and sat next to her. "Let me just see what's happening with your temperature, okay?"

Libby nodded and sipped at her juice. "I hot."

"Yeah, I think you are." I turned the device on,

waited for it to boot up, and placed the nozzle gently in her ear. "Hold still a minute, baby girl."

"'Kay." She stopped swinging her legs, and I smiled at her.

Once the thermometer beeped, I pulled it away. 102.6°F. Shit. By this point, I was pretty sure she had an ear infection. The last thing I was willing to do was get my vet supplies out and check myself. I'd been filled with horror when Davis had suggested I do something similar and have a go at diagnosis the last time she'd felt under the weather.

While Libby could be a cheeky monkey, veterinary medicine and human medicine did not mix.

"Do you want to watch some TV while I go check on Daddy?"

"Yes, pease." She jumped on down and headed to the TV. There was no need to follow. She knew exactly how to use the remote and the number of her favorite channel. Kids legit were so tech savvy that it made my brain spin.

"Hey, Davis," I said, just louder than a whisper. I needed to wake him but not freak him the hell out. I knelt on the mattress next to him. He was on his side, hair mussed and eyes closed.

His hand appeared from under the blanket and snatched me by the waist. I half fell on him, snort-laughing. "Oomph." His gaze met mine, and a sleepy smile followed.

"Morning, handsome."

I eased back so I could see his face better. "Morning, yourself. Feel better?" I swept hair that had flopped in his eyes out of the way.

"Yeah, thanks." He stretched despite me being spread almost on top of him. "Did I have long?"

"Almost two hours."

"Libby?"

"She's awake."

Davis nodded. "Best get my ass into gear then, huh."

My lips grazed his before I pulled back to give him space to move. "She still has a temp. It's gone up to 102.6 degrees."

"Shit, really?" He became immediately more alert.

My heart constricted. "Yeah."

"Right." Sitting up, he stretched out fully, then was out of bed and getting dressed.

"Hey, slow down. She's just had some juice and is in front of the TV. I really think it's her ear, maybe an infection. I remember Jenna telling me one of the boys had one a few years back and said how shit it all was, but it's easily treated."

I stood in front of Davis and took his hands in

mine. When his eyes searched mine, relief seemed to hit its mark, and his shoulders relaxed a fraction. "Okay."

"I'll go call the clinic and let them know we need an appointment, okay?"

"Yeah, thanks."

I backed away to make the call, checking on Libby in the process. She lay on the floor, her gaze intent on the big screen, a car in her hand that she was mindlessly rolling on the hardwood.

They managed to fit her in at eight thirty, so it meant Davis could attempt to calm down a little. My gut twisted every time he was in distress; add in Libby being so out of sorts, and my gut was something akin to a damn roller coaster leaping off the tracks and going on a joy ride.

There were zero regrets in the choices I'd made over the last couple of years. Having Davis and Libby in my life and loving them was as instinctive as breathing. But that didn't mean the anxiety riding me in such situations was a good feeling. Stepping up to be there for Davis, though, offered the perfect distraction—until my phone rang.

"Shit." In my peripheral vision, I saw Davis glance in my direction. His gaze fell when he realized who was on the line. "Hello, this is Scott."

"Hey, Scott, it's Daisy. We have an emergency heading in. A cat's been hit by a car."

I closed my eyes briefly, then cast my gaze on Davis while responding, "Okay, thanks. I'll be there in ten." Hitting End, it was impossible to ignore the guilt sitting heavily on my chest.

"It's okay. Honestly."

A grimace fell over my face. "I know but—"

"You have animals who need you."

"But you and Libby need me too."

Davis moved toward me, a small smile flitting across his lips. "I do, but even though you can't come with me, I know you're still here. Plus, like you said yourself, it's probably just an ear infection, which will suck for her, but it's easily fixed, right?"

"Right," I begrudgingly admitted, leaning toward him and pressing my lips to his. When I pulled away, I allowed myself a moment to read his face as best as I could, making sure he wasn't really pissed. Only understanding was there. "Thank you."

He nudged me away. "Get your butt into gear and go and save an elephant or something."

I snorted. "A cat.'"

"A cat then, but an elephant would be cooler."

I stepped away to grab my things, then quickly left after giving Libby a cuddle goodbye.

CHAPTER THREE

DAVIS

"I'll catch you later. You're working late tonight, right?"

Scott gave a nod, barely perceptible from beneath the layer of covers he was still under. It was only five, and the sun still had a couple of hours before it would rise.

I pressed a kiss to the top of his head and left. Last night was the first in seemingly forever that Libby had slept all the way through. The antibiotics had kicked in and cleared up her ear infection toward the end of last week, but her body had got into the crappy habit of waking up multiple times.

All three of us weren't quite recovered, but I hoped last night's good sleep was an indication we'd all be functioning on full cylinders again soon.

This coming weekend, Scott and I were due to head away. Up until this morning, I hadn't been convinced that it would be possible. Just maybe, though, it could happen. Lord knew we could do with a break, and Libby loved spending time with her cousins and aunt, so it was a treat for her too.

But I still had the day to get through, plus I needed to book the motel for tomorrow night.

The empty café lit with the growing morning light was a peaceful start to the day. With the sounds of the refrigerator and freezer buzzing, the coffee machine warming up, and the gas hob on, there was a gentle backdrop, allowing me to get my head straight.

Jasper was due in at six thirty and Jenna at eleven. Between the three of us, we'd happily handle the busy periods, and I'd have time after the lunchtime rush to sort some orders and make sure everything was set for the weekend.

All being well, we planned to leave tomorrow around lunchtime. It meant we could check in to our motel, freshen up, and hopefully I could get Scott revved up enough to give him something to be thinking about while we were out. We'd then head back midmorning on Sunday to pick up our girl.

The sound of the front door unlocking and being pushed open alerted me to the time. While I'd done what I'd set out to achieve so far, the morning had sped by crazy fast.

"Hey, boss man."

I grinned as Jasper popped his head around the open doorway. "Morning."

"You're looking a little more human today. Better night?"

I bobbed my head and cast him a smile. "I looked that bad, huh?"

A quiet snort led to "Well, not quite the words I would have chosen, but, pretty much, yeah." He righted himself, his eyes lighting up. "Does this mean tomorrow's on? Are you guys able to head out?"

Screw it. "Yeah, let's do it." While I hadn't had the final conversation with Scott, I knew he was looking forward to a night out. And when I'd confirmed it was to a gay club, he'd been so damn intrigued and genuinely excited, there was no way I wanted to miss out on him checking the place out.

"Hell yes! You need the details of the motel?"

I shook my head. "I've still got them, thanks. I'll jump online in a while and book a room." I placed some ingredients in the fridge, then headed out to the front, Jasper hot on my heels. "I know it's all last minute, but you can still grab a lift with us tomorrow if you want?" I went about checking the coffee machine as Jasper flipped the sign to Open.

"Nah, thanks. I have Monday off, so thought I'd make a long weekend of it. Plus, you never know how lucky I might get." His brows jumping up and down had me shaking my head.

"There is that, I suppose." It had been a long time since I'd been in the position to hook up for a night of screwing with anyone, and I had to admit, relief that I wouldn't be in that position again raced through me. Scott's fine ass, his sometimes-wicked personality, teamed with the random bouts of shyness and sweetness were more than enough to keep my heart and my dick happy.

Forever, I hoped.

Jasper sighed, drawing my attention back to him.

"Everything okay over there?"

He was lowering the last few chairs and stools. "Yeah, just thinking it must be all kinds of fabulous to be so loved up and have a man like Scott keeping you warm at night." A forlorn look of longing appeared on his face. Surely he was too damn young to be wishing for forever, right? I internally shrugged, fully aware it would be a dick move for me to say as much, as what the hell did I know beyond that I was lucky as hell to have found Scott?

"Yeah, it sure is," I finally decided on. "You're still so young and have plenty of time for settling down." I thought back to what I was like in my twenties. I'd had no problem with experimenting and getting my fill whenever I wanted.

"Yeah, I know. I suppose I'm just frustrated."

"Ahh." I got it. This was not the job for him. I imagined between his degree going to waste, not following his dreams and all that, plus not having a warm body to lick whenever he felt the urge, it made everything he didn't have seem like one giant hurdle. "You know, I was a hell of a lot older than you when I met Scott." He side-eyed me, and I put up my hand, intending to appease. "*But* I also know of couples who met their significant other as young as seventeen and are still together. What I'm trying to say is, it'll happen. You're a smart guy. Good-looking and have a good heart."

He fluttered his lashes at me, ridiculously so, and cupped his chin just as Ted from the bar down the street entered. "Aww, you think I'm a gorgeous genius, huh? That's so damn cute."

I rolled my eyes and snorted, flicking a smile in Ted's direction. "I'm heading in the back; perhaps you can stroke Jasper's ego for a while, Ted."

Ted's smile turned into a mischievous grin. "Ooh, there's nothing I'd love more. Not sure my gorgeous husband would approve though, but what he doesn't know...." He trailed off into laughter.

"There's no hope for anyone in this town with you two around," I threw out as I headed into the kitchen.

"You know I like to bring a little color and charisma into this old town, Davis. Speaking of, I wanted to talk to you about my and Jason's anniversary. We're going to have a party and wanted help with catering."

I opened my mouth to answer, only to be cut off by Ted as he continued. "I know, I know you don't cater, but this is me. And you know I know how you know how special I am and important in your world."

Jasper snorted while I looked on bug-eyed. Nothing about what flew out of Ted's mouth should surprise me anymore. He certainly had a way with words and knew how to complicate the shit out of something. I dropped my head in defeat. There was no way he'd take no for an answer. It was easier to simply give in and roll with it. "Fine, but—"

"I knew I could win you over." He strode toward me and pulled me into a hug.

I begrudgingly patted his back to Jasper's peals of laughter. "Yeah, yeah. Just give me dates, and we'll sit down soon and get it squared away."

He grinned big and planted a kiss on my cheek. "You're a darl." Yep, since he moved into town with his husband, not long after Scott moved to Kirkby, he truly had caused a stir. Admittedly, I liked him the more for it. I had no idea how Jason, his much younger, taller, and more serious husband put up with him. I was always exhausted after a session of drinks and chats.

But they were both good people. And it did add an extra layer of comfort knowing there was a slow-growing number of people in our small town who identified as LGBTQ.

I waved him off and let Jasper sort out his order, wondering what craziness he'd be asking for to celebrate his anniversary.

"ARE YOU SURE YOU'VE GOT EVERYTHING?"

I made sure I didn't roll my eyes at Scott. Just once, or maybe two or three times, I'd forgotten something that had proved "essential" when going on a trip. It didn't mean I'd forget every damn time. "I'm sure," I finally answered, keeping the annoyance from my voice.

Last night Libby had woken up a couple of times, so our peace had gone. Without a temp, and her waking up smiley and seemingly fine, we'd opted to still go. This was after Jenna put pressure on and told us to "get a grip and go and have fun."

It meant we were both tired and testy. And packing Libby's stuff, even though she was staying just a few minutes away and Jenna had a key to our house, always seemed to add a layer of stress. As well as the fact we were leaving Libby for the night.

We did need to get ourselves on the road though and start to unwind. The last thing either of us wanted was to have an argument over nothing and ruin our weekend.

When Scott didn't reply, I shifted my gaze in his direction. His right brow was quirked high.

"What?" I asked innocently.

His left brow joined the right, and his mouth twitched.

"Bollocks to you." I grinned and threw one of

Libby's soft toys at his head. He caught it before it hit him square in the face.

"You're so going to get it tonight."

My gut clenched, my dick twinged, and any concern of an argument went flying out the window along with any pure thoughts. "I have to wait till tonight?" I hefted Libby's bag on my shoulder.

"At this rate, yes. Get your ass into gear." Scott threw the stuffed bunny back at me. I wasn't so quick, and it smacked me on my nose. His laughter followed me out of Libby's room.

"Get *your* ass into gear," I mumbled before an "Oomph" fell from me as Scott grabbed me from behind, wrapping me in his arms.

"You say something?" His warm breath swept across my ear, and I forced myself not to melt in his arms. Where was the fun in making it too easy?

"Me?" I shrugged, enjoying his lips pressing against my neck. "What answer do you want me to give to make sure you keep doing that?" The kisses stopped as I felt his lips part into a smile. A pinch on my butt swiftly followed.

"Get a move on so we don't get there too late."

I followed his movement as he brushed past me, heading to collect our overnight bag. My eyes stuck to his ass for as long as possible.

God, I was a horny fuck.

It wasn't like we didn't go at it whenever we had the chance, but parenting was a hard gig, especially with Libby's ear infection and all our sleepless nights.

Making my way to the TV room, I debated how much we really needed to go out clubbing. Weren't we past it? A night for the two of us in a motel sounded better and better. We'd be able to eat dinner in bed, spend a stupid amount of money by raiding the minibar, and watch a dodgy porno or two.

It sounded pretty damn spectacular to me.

I shook those thoughts from my head.

"Come on, pretty girl. It's time to head to see your tearaway cousins." It was all lies. Libby was the rebel of the bunch. As the youngest, she had the boys wrapped around her little finger. She was already talking them into doing stupid shit. Christ knew how much worse it would get over the years.

"Yay!" She jumped to her feet.

"Grab your bag." I indicated toward the bag at the door. She'd had the responsibility to shove any toys that she wanted to take with her in there. It was bulging at the seams and was due to explode Disney princesses and Transformers at any moment.

"'Kay," she said, scooting on over to heave it up.

"You need a hand?"

"Nope. I gots two." She held up both, still somehow grasping the handles of her bag, and strained under its weight.

Amused, I shook my head. "Come on. Scott will be waiting for us."

Low and behold, the car doors were open, our bag stowed, and he stepped out to take Libby's bags.

Before long, Libby was strapped in and we were finally leaving. I glanced at the time. Only forty-five minutes later than planned. I was impressed.

We managed to finally get on the road heading out of town after another thirty minutes. I glanced over at Scott, who was driving, and exhaled loudly, a smile following closely behind.

"You're feeling relaxed already, huh." He darted his eyes my way, his gaze flicking to my mouth before he returned his focus ahead. It was generally a quiet section of road and hopefully would stay that way until we were thirty miles or so out of the city.

I shifted in my seat and stretched. "I really am." A quick glance over my shoulder reminded me we were child-free, which always took some getting used to. "What playlist do you want to listen to?" There were a few road-trip worthy ones.

"No dodgy nineties."

I snorted. "That was that one time." A playlist I'd downloaded from iTunes last year had had me delving into the days of indie from the nineties. Scott had threatened to hack into my account and cancel it if he had to listen to "Wonderwall" one more time. Though hack was a complete elaboration since we knew each other's passwords.

Yep, we were *that* couple.

He gave me a hard stare.

"Fine." I relented and put on a covers mix. He rewarded me with a wink.

"I haven't seen Tanner all week. Everything okay?"

"Yeah." I nodded. "Tanner's started a new remodel so is snowed under."

"Have you heard they want a new dog?"

I shook my head. "When did that happen?"

"Carter mentioned it on Monday, so is obsessively searching and looking at availability. You know how he gets."

I really did. He liked mapping everything out and overthinking at times. Rex had come easily, since originally he was Tanner's dog. But throw Carter in the mix and it would become an operation of sorts. I laughed. "It's probably good Tanner's so busy. Being surrounded by printouts and probably pros and cons of a breed would drive him insane."

"I'd pay to see that," Scott said, a smile curving his lips. With that, he reached out, took my hand, and placed it on his firm thigh. What I wouldn't give to relive my more reckless days and go down on him while he was driving. Responsibility sucked ass, but not in the mind-blowing orgasm kind of way.

The drive was easy. Even navigating through the city to the motel that was only about a mile from the club proved straightforward. After the comical wide-eyed stare from the motel manager when he passed us our key and watched Scott hug my waist from behind, we were settled in the room, and I wasn't quite sure who launched on who first.

Our legs tangled, his still stuck in his jeans, while my arm was wedged in my tee. "Shit." I laughed the word. "I need help."

Scott paused, his mouth leaving my skin. Heated eyes connected with mine as he stood and removed his jeans fully. Rather than helping me with my tee, he instead latched on to my ankles and dragged me so I was on the edge of the bed, my legs dangling off. Sure I looked like a tangled, flaying pretzel, I stilled. "What are you—"

When he licked up my thigh and all but swallowed me down, the question seemed moot. Instead, "Holy dick" followed by a deep groan left my mouth.

His laugh vibrated around me and had me bucking up from the bed. With only one hand free and having no desire to tear my focus from Scott's hot mouth, I eased myself back to the mattress and tangled my fingers in his hair with a grunt and a sigh. "You trying to kill me?" I panted. Laughter with a mouthful of cock was too much for me to handle.

He pulled away, a deep, full laugh breaking free. He looked so sexy like this. Eyes full of lust. Lips swollen and glistening. And a huge smile on his mouth.

"I love you so damn much."

His smile became impossibly wide as he angled over me and helped me remove my T-shirt. Once released, I wrapped my arms around him. His naked flesh against mine was one of the best sensations ever. Warmth, heat, and comfort, all tangled up with the love that filled us both. A gentle press of his lips to mine and I sighed, content. I pressed a little harder and tilted my head slightly so I could speak. Scott lifted his head and pressed his weight on his forearms.

"I want you in my mouth and riding my fingers."

He reacted exactly as I imagined. He jumped up

and urged me further up the bed. Barely in position, I chuckled as he lay on his side, his groin in my face and his tongue lapping at my erection. Needless to say, my chuckle cut off abruptly as I cupped his backside and urged him to my mouth.

With licks, fingers, and some of the best head he'd ever given, we were both blowing our load within fifteen minutes. In my exhaustion and orgasm haze, I patted myself on the back for lasting so long. Scott's ability to find and stimulate my P spot was worthy of freaking accolades. If there'd been a national award or some shit, screw his mortification, I would have nominated him quicker than it took for him to zero in on the magic area itself that had me screaming like a deity.

"If I could love you any more, I would after that," I said breathily as he scooted around to lie in my arms.

He trailed his fingers across my chest and chuckled, his breath brushing across my skin causing goose bumps. "Right back at you." He grazed a kiss on my cheek. "Shower and nap?"

The thought of getting up made me groan. "I'm comfortable."

"Me too." Then the bastard stuck his fingers in my side and tickled. Hard.

"Ahh." I shot out of bed, almost taking his eye out in the process as my elbow flew close to his face. "Fuck. Fine." I stood and slapped his ass for good measure, enjoying the curse and grunt that followed me into the bathroom.

CHAPTER FOUR

SCOTT

So this was what freedom looked like. I was only a couple of drinks in, but I still had to forcibly work at not staring with a slack jaw. Davis, by my side, helped me refocus. Gentle circles looped on the arch of my back, his silent way of offering me both comfort and reassurance.

Everything about the club was way out of my comfort zone. But riding alongside the awkwardness that had hit hard when I'd stepped inside was incredible familiarity. The place itself offered a bubble of protection to every out-and-proud individual in the joint.

And that right there was something extraordinary in my sheltered gay life.

"You need something stronger?" Davis indicated

my beer.

"No, thanks." While I knew tonight was about letting go and taking some time out, I had no desire to get shitfaced. Not only did I have a date with my man when we got back to the motel later, but with the openness of the club, and not needing to refrain from showing Davis how I felt publicly, I didn't want to forget a moment.

Lightness filled my chest, expanding and making me lighter, braver. "Dance with me." It didn't matter that the music was some modern dance crap. What mattered was having Davis close to me.

He moved and stood before me, his grin wide, his eyes filled with what I knew was love. "You mean I get to dance with the hottest guy in the place?" A laugh followed, his hand moving to my waist. "Hell yes." He downed his beer, indicating I should do the same. I did so willingly and allowed myself to be led to the dance floor and the many gyrating bodies. Jasper's included.

Once we were situated under the flashing lights, my eyes remained on Davis. Both his hands settled on my waist, and our bodies moved, perhaps a little too slow for the beat, but in the hour we'd been here, one thing had been made crystal clear: anything goes.

My smile was impossible to contain. I embraced the freedom the club offered, shed the restriction everyday life in a predominantly straight world locked me in to. And I loved every single moment of it.

The track changed to something sexier, though with a solid beat. Davis tugged me closer, his lips skimming mine. I welcomed his mouth, luxuriated in the familiarity of the touch in the strange setting. Awareness of many bodies around me rippled through my brain. The knowledge fueled me on, had me sucking on his tongue.

There was no chance I'd miss out on a single moment of the luxury of kisses in public without fear. Exhilarated, I clamped my hands on his ass.

Davis groaned deeply. I smiled against his mouth, and he soon grinned back.

"You're so hot, baby." His words brushed against me, and I hauled his groin closer to mine, letting him know just how hot I was for him.

"All for you."

"Is it too early to leave?" he said with a mischievous glint in his eyes.

I threw my head back and laughed loudly, only to freeze when a body rubbed up behind me. Still frozen, my eyes widen as I stared at Davis in panic.

Davis nudged me around, effectively turning me so I was away from the person who'd thought it would be okay to attach themselves to me.

"He's mine, and neither of us share." His words sounded light, but by the hard set of his shoulders, I knew he wasn't messing around.

"Sorry." The guy, a little shorter than Davis, held up his hand in defense, a crooked smile playing on his lips. He was cute and young, maybe even ten years younger than me. He was also seriously built, his shoulders wide and massively toned. An arm wrestle with the guy would have me pushed into the floor. "I've been watching you for a while. Thought we could have some fun."

I kept my mouth shut, more than happy for Davis to take the lead on this. I was a novice to gay clubs and had no idea of the etiquette. The last thing I wanted was to insult someone and start something.

"I understand," Davis said. "My guy here is hot, but no one touches him but me. He's mine."

Heat licked through me at his possessive words. Davis was so chilled most of the time that he was almost horizontal. Only occasionally did this side of him come out. There was no denying my body loved it, and my heart bouncing around in my chest was a sure giveaway his words got to me.

"And how about you?" the guy said, seeming to have forgotten Davis's first statement about not sharing.

I froze before angling forward. "Hell no."

Davis's laugh washed over me, his lips finding purchase against my neck.

The man before us laughed lightly, nothing but humor in the sound. "I get it, all good." He stuck his hand out. "Name's Ian."

I eyed his hand a moment, then relaxed, reading the smile on his face as genuine. "Scott." I gripped his hand for a beat, then indicated toward Davis. "And this is my Davis."

Ian grinned at my ownership. "Gotcha." He placed his palm in Davis's. "Good to meet you both." He glanced around the full floor. "Sorry to stop you guys from dancing." He spoke loudly over the music and the crowd of voices.

"All good," Davis answered, his hand trailing down my arm until he held my hand. "I think we need a drink anyway."

Ian nodded. While the same smile spread across his mouth, it seemed to slip a little, this time not quite touching his eyes.

"You can join us for a drink if you want," I offered with a shrug, and Davis squeezed my hand lightly. I glanced at him, worried he was pissed. He wasn't. Perhaps he'd seen what I'd seen.

"Yeah, sure." Ian's eyes widened, his smile relaxing. "If you don't mind."

"Nope, it's all good."

Davis led the way off the dance floor, my hand still clasped in his and Ian trailing behind us. On the way, I saw Davis indicate to Jasper that we were heading to the bar. He simply grinned as he ground himself against a guy who easily had forty pounds on him, mainly muscle, and stood at least six inches taller.

At the bar, Davis ordered our drinks and offered to buy Ian one. He accepted gratefully, and then we left the main room for a section of the club where there was seating and the music was quieter so conversation was possible.

"I am really sorry for my lame attempt to hit on you guys." A grimace creased Ian's otherwise wrinkle-free forehead. He seriously was young. A sigh followed as he took the drink. Though the sigh seemed one of small relief.

I turned my focus to Davis when he started to speak. "All good. I know lots of guys are into sharing, but Scott and I are exclusive."

Ian bobbed his head in understanding. He

gnawed on his bottom lip a moment, his eyes glancing around the room before trailing back to us. "Yeah." He shrugged. "I sort of figured that. It's why I came to you guys in the first place." He gave a small shrug while confusion swept through me. Before I could ask, he continued. "There's been a guy hassling me since I came in. I told him I knew you both, so I sort of escaped."

"Hassling you how?" I sat up a little straighter and was tempted to glance around, but instead focused on Ian.

"Just a dick who struggles to hear no."

"Did you not speak to one of the security guys?" Davis asked.

Ian shook his head, saying, "Nope. He didn't get handsy or anything. I've been coming to this place for the past couple of months. I don't live far, so it's just an easy visit, you know. Plus there's usually a really nice crowd here, guys who at least want a conversation before hooking up, you know?"

I really didn't. This world was as alien as it was eye-opening to me.

"I keep seeing the guy around. He tries it on every single time. The first time I was tempted. We chatted, and I may have let him shove his tongue down my throat and his finger up my ass." He started laughing when his eyes landed on me. Yeah, my eyes had sprung wide open at his candor. His smile dropped a moment later. "So yeah, I told him thanks, but I didn't actually want to fuck that night. Wasn't looking at taking anyone home. He finally backed off, and since then, he's just there, you know…." Another sip of his drink and he seemed to shrug off the growing agitation that had lifted his voice when he spoke. "So anyway. Sorry I annoyed you out there. But I kinda figured you were safe, you know?"

Sensing Davis's eyes on me, I glanced in his direction. Whoever this dickhead was who kept hitting on Ian sounded like a creep. My lips tilted up at Davis a little, and he winked at me before refocusing on Ian.

"After this drink, we're going to hit the dance floor. You're good to come with."

"Really?" Ian's eyes lit up. The innocence on his face didn't quite match the ripped body, but I was hardly one to be casting judgment. What the hell did I know?

"Yeah," I added. "Or if you want to leave, we can walk you out to get a cab or an Uber or something?"

A wide smile broke free on Ian. "Dancing would be great. I look forward to getting out once a week, blowing off some steam. Sometimes a dance floor is all I want, you know?" He downed his drink. "Work can be a fuck, so it's good to wind down."

I eyed his tight tee over his larger-than-average muscles, wondering what he did for a living and if those muscles were part of it. I also wondered why Ian didn't kick the other dude's ass.

Davis, as if reading my mind, said, "Yeah, it is. We've a little girl and both work long hours, so we know all too well how important it is to get away." Davis placed his hand on my thigh and squeezed a little. Heat touched my cheeks at the contact. "We don't do this enough, that's for sure. What is it you do?"

"Oh wow, a daughter, huh. Bet she keeps you busy." Genuine interest lifted his tone. "And I'm a nurse. I work at the local hospital here, in the emergency room."

Huh. I cast a glimpse at Davis and saw his eyes widen a little.

"No shit," he said. "Honestly, I'd never have guessed it." His eyes roamed Ian's broad chest. I got it. I did. I coughed lightly and raised my brow in Davis's direction. He looked at me and laughed. "As if you weren't doing and thinking the same." He rolled his eyes at me. Bastard was spot-on. Asshole.

A snort had us both looking at Ian. "I like to work out." A shit-eating grin greeted us. "But I'm also a healer and a lover." He shrugged. "I don't do aggressive bullshit."

"Yeah, for sure. Scott here is a veterinarian. Owns his own practice." My chest puffed out a little at the pride I heard in his voice. "Though he can be a real asshole as well as a healer." His loud laugh followed.

"Hey." I quirked my brow at him.

"What?" I didn't buy his innocence. "Just saying it as I—"

"Yeah, yeah. Keep it up and you'll not be seeing my damn asshole tonight." The words were out of my mouth before I could stop them. Davis's eyes sprang wide in shocked amusement. We both knew it was rare for me to say anything like that in public. In the bedroom, hell yes. Davis quite liked my dirty mouth, but despite the friendliness of Kirkby, I would never have felt comfortable enough to say anything remotely like that.

Restricting myself and how I felt about Davis so I wouldn't draw attention to us was draining. I'd known that, lived it, but until this moment, I hadn't fully comprehended just how liberating it was to live so openly.

Kirkby needed a gay bar or club. Stat. I was sure I

could talk Ted into it.

Ian and Davis's mutual laughter had me smiling, and had Davis leaning into me and asking, "What's going on in that head of yours?"

I answered with a small brush of my lips to his. When I pulled away, I was grinning. "Gay night at Ted's once a month until we can talk him into opening one up."

Davis snorted. "Not sure Kirkby is quite ready for that yet." He angled his head, a soft smile on his lips. "But he wouldn't take too much convincing."

"You guys are so adorable and loved up." Ian's voice broke us apart and left us rolling our eyes.

"You see, Scott, someone else thinks you're adorable."

I edged my middle finger to my cheek and scratched up and down, causing a snort from Ian and a grin from Davis.

"Come on." Davis knocked back his drink before standing and hauling me to my feet. "Let's go dance. They're finally playing something half decent."

I grinned, hearing a dodgy nineties song that I'd previously mocked him for. I glanced down at Ian. Uncertainty played across his features as he flicked his glance at us. "You coming?" I asked. The poor guy needed a break. The creep who'd been giving him a hard time sounded like a piece of work, and Ian looked like he needed a bit more alcohol and needed to dance his anxiety out of his system. "We've got you."

Davis squeezed my hand at my words and his heat pressed against me. I knew what they meant to us. And sometimes, extending a helping hand to someone who seemed like they needed a break, was by far not the hardest thing to accomplish.

Ian's eyes brightened as he stood, happiness on his face as he stepped a little closer and then followed us out.

Yeah, there was no way I'd be sharing Davis's body with anyone, but we could both afford to share a bit of kindness.

Before long, a fine layer of sweat coated my skin and my stomach hurt from laughing so much. My barely there abs had loosened up over the past couple of years. Between the dancing and the snort-laughing over Jasper and Ian's ridiculous moves, it was no wonder I ached in the best of ways.

I glanced at my watch, aware they'd slowed the music down to a sexy, slow beat. Eyes widening at the time, I wondered how it had passed by so quickly.

"You ready to head out?" Davis wrapped himself

up in me, his mouth by my ear. He followed up with his lips caressing my neck.

Gooseflesh pebbled my skin, and I smiled as I held him close. "Can do."

"Should I let Jasper know?"

A quick glance in his direction had me laughing. He and Ian were doing completely OTT dance moves, both cackling with laughter. They'd hit it off immediately, but I hadn't seen anything beyond fun flirtation between the two of them. "I suppose." Neither of us wanted to leave Jasper high and dry. I knew he came to the city to party at least once a month so was used to the scene, but discomfort layered my gut at him being by himself. The friends he'd expected to meet hadn't shown.

He was still so damn young.

It didn't take long before we were settled in our room after dropping Ian at home, despite his protests that he could walk, and saying goodnight to Jasper, who'd headed into his room singing and stumbling a little.

"I'm beat." I stretched, contemplating grabbing a shower before I slept. I sniffed my shirt and scrunched my nose in distaste.

Davis's snort caught my attention. "You smell that good, huh?"

I grinned, reached out and tugged him to me. "You want a sniff?" My brows bobbed up and down.

He shook his head. "Maybe after a shower."

"What, you don't want my manly smell?"

"Is that what we're calling your dancing-for-hours sweat stink?"

I laughed. "Maybe." I pressed closer toward him. "A shower will wake me up a little so you can suck me off." My grin was wide as I finished speaking.

"Wow, feeling generous, huh? Letting me wrap my mouth around you."

I groaned at his words, wanting nothing more than for him to do just that. "Do a good enough job and make me see double and I may just ride you after too." My hand sought out his bulge and I grinned when I found him hard.

"You riding me?" Heat flared in his gaze, and I was sure my own need mirrored his perfectly. "I think you best get your ass into the shower. Make you see double?" He snorted and shook his head. "Screw that, Scott. I'll make you see stars."

Lust burned through my veins as I all but dragged Davis to the shower while trying to undress the both of us. It was only after stumbling when I caught my foot in my jeans that I figured it was best to strip myself first before I did myself damage.

"Hurry up." His mouth latched on to mine as soon as he finished speaking. Davis was a hell of a kisser, and my mouth attached to his was one of my favorite things ever. Need unfurled in my gut, my cock jutting out and rock-hard. I pulled back enough to tear off my socks and turn on the shower.

"Fuck." I gasped as the cold spray hit me.

"Holy crap, that's cold."

Laughter rolled through me, Davis's chuckle following before I silenced him with a kiss. With his tongue caressing mine, our lips pressing and in sync, I sighed happily, especially as the water finally heated.

When Davis pulled away, I grumbled, hating the loss of his mouth. His words silenced me. "You looked so hot tonight. In your element." His eyes searched mine, his affection shining through. "I loved seeing you like that." He pressed his mouth to my nipple, sucked and bit before lowering down, trailing kisses along the way. "Loved kissing you whenever I wanted." His strong hand cradled me. "Loved seeing you not worrying about anyone seeing how much you want me."

I groaned as he took me in his mouth. "I'll always want you." Truth and fire lit my words. This man was my everything. My fucking world. The flat of his tongue stroked over me, lapped along my vein, and my legs wobbled. My hand found purchase on his head and I paused him a moment. When his eyes found mine, his mouth looking so damn hot as it framed my dick, I spoke my truth. "You're everything. I love you."

Unwavering, his gaze remained fixed on mine as he bobbed, licked, and swallowed. Flashes of heat and need registered in his eyes, and I knew damn well he felt exactly how I did.

Through everything, not once did I ever doubt Davis or his love. Him shifting had my eyes widening a fraction before my eyes rolled. The fucker. "Holy fuck. Holy shit. What the—" Delicious pressure and a sensation beyond what I'd ever experienced before wrapped around my glans. Tears sprang in my eyes, and my gasping and groaning echoed around the bathroom. My back arched, and I managed to pry my eyes open and look down to see Davis's nose pressed against my skin. The knowledge that he was deep-throating barely had time to register before numbness battled with every nerve ending, which seemed to flare. Shaking took over my limbs as those stars he'd promised flashed before my eyes. I shuddered as the end of my orgasm rippled through me, and Davis managed to detach himself just as my legs gave way and I slid to the shower floor, landing on my ass.

He wrapped me in his arms as I pressed my forehead to his chest. Unable to speak, I focused on breathing and getting the shudders wrecking my body under control.

"Okay?" His voice was croaky, sounding rough as hell. "You're not going to die on me, right?" His slight laughter was scratchy.

"Mmm... 'kay" was all I could manage. Taking a deep breath, I also sniffed deeply. Despite the water still beating down, I could pick up Davis's scent. The small smell of sweat still clung to his skin along with his aftershave. My lips touched his chest, then his neck before I angled away, a sloppy grin on my face.

My eyes met his, mine filled with wonder, his filled with heat and a hell of a lot of satisfaction. "Can you stand?" he asked.

"I think so. Might need help though."

He laughed as he got up from his knees and helped pull me to my feet.

Once as steady as I could manage on my feet, we washed each other down, sharing kisses as we went.

"So," I finally asked when his mouth was at my throat, and once more I was full-mast, "deep-throating, huh?"

"Ha." He winced a little at the harsh sound and swallowed thickly.

Concern had me cupping his cheek. "Don't get me wrong, that was quite possibly the best orgasm you've ever given me."

"Ever?" he croaked. "Even better than—"

I shook my head. Heat rushed through me at the memory of the weekend we'd spent worshipping each other. He didn't need to continue for me to know what time he was talking about. "Not sure if anything could top that whole weekend. But," I added, "that blow job was completely unexpected."

His grin was addictive. It lit his eyes and spread his mouth wide. "Yeah?" A small touch on my junk followed his gravelly question. "You ready to dry off?"

I nodded as my hips jerked against him. "So ready."

"Sweet."

A quick squeeze of my ass followed before he passed me a towel and we half-assed dried. Tension thrummed through me; I was more than eager to take this to the bedroom. Keen to feel him deep inside me, I threw the damp towel in the shower and tugged at his hand.

CHAPTER FIVE

DAVIS

DESPITE TIREDNESS FROM A LATE NIGHT BATTLING FOR control, I felt refreshed and couldn't keep the smirk from my face as we drove home. We hadn't fallen asleep until well past three this morning. I'd woken at five-ish wanting more of Scott's heat, and we'd only caught snippets of sleep after that.

A loud yawn from Scott had my own escaping.

I glanced over. The smile he sported looked all levels of incredible on him. In our time together, I wasn't quite sure I'd ever seen him appear so relaxed. The thought pinched my heart.

"You doing okay over there?"

Scott nodded and made eye contact. "Yeah. Great, in fact." A quick check of the time on his phone had him saying, "Should be back soon. An afternoon in bed sounds great."

My stomach dipped. We needed to pick up Libby. That meant there was no chance of afternoon naps. "Jenna's expecting us as soon as we get into town." I focused on the road ahead. "You want me to drop you off first?"

"No, I'll come with."

"Okay." My nod was stiff. After a carefree night, the reality of Scott having responsibilities he perhaps never asked for niggled at me. He loved Libby. I was as certain about that as my next breath. But seeing him so free last night and the reality of our life back in the real world had my heart beating erratically and my head spinning.

"What's wrong?" Concern filled Scott's voice.

I remained quiet for a few beats, trying to get my thoughts together. With a heavy sigh and still none the wiser, I shrugged. "Nothing. Ignore me. Just tired I guess." The lie tasted bitter, but there was no chance I could talk anything out or cut through my usual no-bullshit rule when I wasn't a hundred percent sure what my problem was. The niggling doubt of wondering if he was as truly happy as he could be confused the hell out of me. All I was sure of was that my heart felt heavy and something didn't sit right in my gut. Was Scott truly happy?

The relaxed, carefree version of Scott I'd witnessed last night was as wonderful as it was confusing.

Am I holding him back? That thought scratched at my brain, planting an obnoxious seed where I was sure it didn't belong.

All this from the simple knowledge that having a child meant they were priority and naps went out the window.

I seriously wanted to sucker punch myself.

I was not making any sense.

Determined to shove my confusion aside till I could get my head straight, I gave a chin lift toward the sign up ahead. "You want to grab food?"

We were about an hour out, but this morning I hadn't been able to handle anything beyond a black coffee.

"Yeah, sounds good." Scott's hand appeared at the back of my neck, and he gave a gentle squeeze. I risked a glance and hated seeing the deep crease between his brows. I got it. I was as clueless as he was.

I signaled to pull off and quickly found a spot in the parking lot. The diner was a family-owned one and I'd been here a few times. They had great coffee and served good food, or at least they had the last time I'd been here.

Scott's hand found mine as we stepped away from the car, and ease settled the confusing tightness in my body.

"It smells good in here," he mumbled as we entered the diner.

"Got to love cinnamon." With a glance around the room, I spotted a young waitress who was making her way over. Her eyes flicked briefly at our connected hands before she smiled up at us.

"Take a seat wherever, guys. I'll be over with a fresh pot in a few." She indicated the empty coffee pot in her hand.

"Thanks," Scott answered, and I offered a small smile. "Booth?" Scott angled toward me.

"Sounds good."

Scott stopped next to a booth near the window and waited for me to sit.

"Feeling chivalrous this morning, huh."

He snorted. "Yeah, that's me all over."

He slid in next to me rather than sitting opposite. There was no doubt I loved it when he sat beside me. It gave me a chance to touch him. Of course he knew this.

Once positioned, he slid his arm around the back of the booth, his elbow bent, and fingers offering the barest of touches on my neck. Awareness hit me hard, my muscles turning rigid. What the fuck was wrong with me?

"You okay?"

I angled slightly so I could face him better. "Yeah." I forced my limbs to relax. "Just not used to you being into so much PDA." I tilted my head and took the time to let my gaze roam his features. He was so damn handsome and sexy, even when he looked tired and had questions forming in his eyes. "Just to be clear, I love it, and you can touch me whenever and however you want." I grinned and pressed a small kiss to his parted mouth.

He pulled back, his eyes sparkling with mischief. "Yeah? However?"

"Well—"

"Coffee?" The young waitress interrupted my response.

"Yes, please," I answered, tearing my eyes away from Scott to focus on her.

"Both of you?"

"That'll be good, thanks." Scott turned over his mug and smiled.

"Do you know what you're having or do you need more time?"

"Sorry. I got distracted." I quickly picked up the menus, passing one to Scott.

"Understandable." She threw us both a shy smile. "I'll give you a few."

"Thanks," Scott said. When she left, he turned to me. "What's good here?"

"Other than you?" Humor laced my words.

Scott rolled his eyes, which was better than the pretend gagging I expected from him at my cheesy response. "I'm a given," he deadpanned. "And I'm also hungry."

"There are children and respectable people trying to eat in this establishment." The high-pitched voice cut through our teasing, snapping both of our attention in the woman's direction.

So focused on Scott, I hadn't even spotted the older woman reach our table's side. Fierce eyes blazed at us, disgust making her appear even uglier. It was a response, a look I'd seen so many times over the years.

She kept going, her chin wobbling as I tuned into what she was saying. "And to think I like to bring my grandchildren here. I'll be speaking to the manager about this. You should be ashamed of yourselves.

The disgusting display you're putting on, it's not natural."

I fought hard against my reaction to simply tell her to fuck off, all too aware her voice was loud and people were staring our way. Meanwhile, Scott was frozen beside me. It was then I noticed he'd removed his arm. I glanced at him, and my heart plummeted at the horror on his face, his eyes focused on the table before us.

Pale and still, he remained silent. Stoic. His reaction lit a fire in me, spurred me to stop this bullshit before it continued.

"I suggest you stop right there." My voice, firm and low, didn't indicate my growing fury. "I didn't realize there was a sign around here instructing its patrons to not show each other affection." I glanced toward the counter and saw the young waitress staring in horror in our direction. "Excuse me, miss, can you come here a moment?"

She nodded and almost ran to our side. "Everything okay here?"

"I believe so. I was just wondering, do you allow couples in here? See them holding hands, maybe stealing the odd kiss here and there?"

Her eyes widened. She cast a fearful glance at the old bat, who amazingly remained quiet, then nodded and offered a tentative smile. "Yes, sir. All the time."

"Excellent. I was just wondering if it was against company policy or anything to do something as outrageous as hold hands, kiss a cheek? Any rules or notices I should know about?" In my periphery, I saw Scott lift his head and focus on me. I reached over and took his hand in mine, placing it on his thigh.

"No, none." She shook her head. "I think if people were, you know, getting it *on*, then the manager might have something to say." Her cheeks pinkened.

"Perfect. That's what I assumed. Thank you." I turned my attention to the old woman, whose face was bright red. "So, ma'am, I'm all for freedom of speech, but hatred, not so much. To make it clear, if it's a right for heterosexuals—you know, you upstanding straight folk—I can pretty much guarantee it is as well for homosexuals, us gays you seem to have taken as a personal insult to you."

"Actually." The waitress edged forward a little, her shoulders back and the pink darkening to a deeper shade. Her voice shook a little as she continued. "Ma'am, if you're disturbing these customers, I'm going to have to ask you to leave."

Pride for this unknown woman swelled in my chest.

"I beg your pardon. You'll ask me to leave—"

"Ma'am, you're causing an unnecessary scene, and attacking customers, verbally or otherwise, will not be tolerated. I'll settle your check."

"Let me," I intervened. "I'd love nothing more than to pay for your meal." I took a quick glance at the waitress's name tag. "Add it to our check, please, Elise."

Elise grinned at me and headed to the till.

"You have a great day." I offered the old woman a tight smile before returning to my menu. "So, have you thought about what you're going to have?" I squeezed Scott's hand lightly, and he looked over at me.

It had been a long time since I'd seen this expression on his face. While color had returned to his cheeks, he looked lost. Haunted. A fresh surge of anger bubbled under the surface. Last night had been amazing. He'd been free, like no other time I'd known before beyond our own home.

Being together in public had its own set of annoyances. Constantly being on guard, not always being free to act our true selves could be exhausting and was beyond unfair and ridiculous.

I'd walked through life with a "screw you" attitude, rarely stepping away from battles and ready to challenge homophobic assholes. Scott hadn't. It was something I was aware of, his comfort and ease, every time we stepped out of our home.

And last night—

That was it. My earlier reaction, the odd doubt that had peeked its unfamiliar head out.

"Can we go?"

Scott's quiet words cut through my thoughts.

Any thought of challenging him and asking him to stay fled when discomfort filled his features. "Yeah. Come on."

He offered a grateful smile and stood. Half expecting him to turn and immediately head to the counter, relief caught my breath when he waited next to the table and reached out to take my hand. I took it willingly, almost desperately needing the contact after the discomfort of the last few minutes.

"Let's go pay and head home," I said.

"After picking up our girl."

I paused midstep and glanced at him. "Yeah," I said, lifting his hand to my mouth and placing a kiss on the back.

After paying and accepting a bag of muffins and two takeout coffees on the house, alongside an embarrassed apology from the waitress, we headed home. The journey was silent, with the exception of the radio playing quietly. As we hit the town's limits, I cleared my throat and asked, "You okay?"

"Yeah." Despite the despondent tone, he reached out and placed his hand on mine, the two resting on my thigh. "It's just shit, right?"

"Pretty much. You know she's nobody and insignificant to us?"

"Yeah." He sighed deeply and looked at me. "It just hits home my own shame, you know?"

As soon as he said those words, understanding registered. "I get it. I know what you've done, what you've said, and who you are now. History needs to stay in the past even though it gives us the opportunity to reflect and be better. But that doesn't mean you should wallow in guilt or shame. Nor does it mean you need to rehash that every time an asshole doesn't know when to keep their mouth shut."

"I know how lucky I am."

I tore my gaze away from the road for a second, relieved to see his face free of self-loathing. "Why's that? Besides you having access to my ass." My focus returned to the road, and my shoulders relaxed.

He chuckled. "Ass access does have a lot to do with it, but Kirkby's sheltered me, us. I know we don't, you know, have full-on sessions out in public or anything."

"'Cause that would get us arrested."

"There's that," he agreed, humor in his voice. "And to be honest, I've held back a little in that way."

I nodded. "I didn't realize how much until yesterday," I admitted.

"What do you mean?"

I glanced in the rearview mirror. With nothing behind me, I signaled to pull over at the small park near the river. Having finally understood my unease, I needed to get this crap out there. Once in Park, I unbuckled and shifted to face him. He mirrored my movement.

"Yesterday when we were out. I've never seen you like that before."

Scott's brows dipped in confusion. "We had drinks and dancing... topped off the evening with you, what wasn't to enjoy?"

I shook my head. "I know. But it was more about how confident you were with me. We don't really have much physical contact when in public at home."

A shadow passed over his features. He swallowed hard before saying, "You don't think I touch you enough?" The shake of his head screamed of confusion.

"Shit, no, it's not even that." I considered my words carefully before I said, "A hell of a lot has happened to you since being in Kirkby. Your whole life has changed."

"Which I love." Determination lit his words, held them strong.

My heart just about burst out of my chest. I didn't know if I was screwing this up and making a big deal of jack shit. All I knew was there was no way I couldn't get this off my chest. "I know you do. And I love my life with you." I reached out and took his hand in mine, needing the contact.

"So what exactly are you getting at?"

A shallow exhale brushed past my lips. "It feels like you're being held back."

"What?" An incredulous note lifted his next words. "What's that meant to mean?"

A slither of guilt threaded through me. "We both know Kirkby is a small-ass town. Yeah, there's a lot of good people who live there, but there's a heap of narrow-minded dickwads too. Yesterday, seeing you behave how you wanted to, to me, your boyfriend, you've never done that before. I don't want you to have to settle is all. Didn't know whether you'd be happier living elsewhere. A city. Somewhere bigger." The words were out, and I wanted to punch myself in the face. It sounded like I was questioning how he felt about me, and that was not what I'd intended.

Sadness clouded Scott's face, taking me by surprise. Since being together, we'd been hacked off a fair few times, but this was different. His being so upset to the point of sadness in his eyes was a whole other ballgame.

After swallowing loudly, he whispered, "Jenna's expecting us," the words barely audible. He shook his head once, straightened in the seat, and focused straight ahead.

Fuck.

"Scott, baby, I wasn't questioning—"

"Davis, I just… just get us to Libby, then home. I can't talk to you about this right now. Please."

Sorrow wasn't even close to the dejection I could all but see radiating off him.

I could be a pushy bastard when I wanted to be, but it clearly wasn't the right time to shove at the moment. Sighing, I concentrated on evening out my breaths before putting the car into gear and heading to his sister's.

CHAPTER SIX

SCOTT

"WHOA, WHAT WAS THAT ALL ABOUT?"

As much as I wanted to avoid Carter, there was no hope. He was like a dog with a bone when he wanted to be. Reluctantly, I glanced over at him. Standing in my office doorway, he looked the epitome of concerned. I blew out a breath. "Sorry. You want to come in and close the door behind you?"

A bear with a bump on his head didn't come close to how ridiculously bad-tempered I'd been all morning. All caused by the despondency riding me hard. Carter hadn't been at work yesterday, else I was sure he would have pinned me down then. Today there was someone here to actually call me on my shit. And Carter was stepping toward the chair in front of my desk, worry radiating off him, to do just that.

"You want to tell me what crawled up your butt?"

"Really?"

His lips rose a little, but when I didn't offer any humor back, the smile slipped from his face. "You were just ridiculous with Nicole. You owe her a box of donuts."

I sighed and sat at my desk. "I know. I'll step out later and get some." Even though that would mean having to go to Davis's café, which I really didn't want to do, but he had the best donuts and pastries. But every time I saw him, worry clenched my gut. Deep down—and honestly, I didn't have to look that deep—I knew he hadn't been questioning us, but his challenge had ruffled me. I was happy here, with Davis and Libby. Even happy at work. But his push at suggesting I wanted or needed more had thrown me for a loop.

The altercation at the coffeehouse with the old dragon lady had not been pleasant and had brought my insecurities out and reminded me what assholes existed in the world. But that hurdle—and I knew there'd be a regular hurdle wearing the face of a prejudiced idiot—wasn't enough to make me unhappy with all that I had in my life.

"So what gives?" Carter took the chair in front of my desk. "I haven't heard anything from you or Davis about this weekend or anything. Something happen there or since you've been back?"

"I really don't want to talk about this."

"Have you talked to Davis about whatever this is?" He waved a hand in my general direction. Before I could respond, he said, "Apparently not."

I wasn't great at keeping my emotions off my face at the best of times, but after an amazing night away, to then have the weird nonargument with Davis—I honestly had no idea what else to call it—I'd gone into avoidance mode. Which then resulted in me owing donuts to my staff.

"Well, if you're not talking to him about this, then spill."

I eyed the door, wondering what my chances of escape were.

"Don't even think it." His words had me flicking my gaze to him. "I know you don't have appointments at all today, and you're in here doing owner stuff."

I quirked my brow at him. "Owner stuff?"

"That's what I said. Now spill. You're not leaving till you get whatever's burning you up off your chest, and if you don't, I'll call in reinforcements."

I blanched at that, thinking of the three possibilities, knowing he either meant Ted, Lauren, or Tanner. None were favorable. "Fine." I cracked my neck from side to side before I told him how great our night had been. I carried on, telling him about the cute stray, Ian, we'd picked up, and then I explained about the coffee shop and the old dragon lady.

He remained silent, allowing me to speak and share my story, offering nods, a few smiles, and then annoyed gasps when I got to the point.

"So what happened with Davis?" He paused a moment, eyeing me carefully. "Are you sure you understood him correctly? I know Davis usually tells it as it is, but sometimes we don't always make ourselves as clear as we should."

"What? About me being held back and miserable?" Heat rushed through my veins at the memory.

"Did he actually say those words?"

I shook my head and attempted to swallow back my unease. "Well, not quite about me being miserable."

"And what about Kirkby?"

"Yes."

"But Kirkby, not him and Libby, right?"

I sighed, the truth right there in front of me. "No,

just about small towns perhaps not always being the most welcoming."

Carter looked as perplexed at my reaction as I did. "So what's the real problem?" He paused before sighing when I didn't respond straight away. "My understanding is that you freaked a little that he was suggesting you weren't what, settled? Happy?" His brows dipped in confusion while I silently agreed with him.

"Panic and overreaction may have been involved." I blew out a heavy breath. "I admit I didn't give much room for him to give a follow-up explanation. And his, what I suppose was protectiveness, made me question whether he thought I was unhappy. That led me to think why he would think I was unhappy. That—"

He raised his hand to stop me. "I get it. I think. Emotions are weird and wonderful things, right?"

A humorless snort escaped as I said, "And some."

"You can't go on buying donuts for people. The staff will sue you if they get diabetes."

I sighed in answer, not having the energy to react to him trying to lighten our conversation, especially as I knew he was right.

"You have to talk—"

"I will." I'd let it stew for two nights, too

caught up in my own emotions to continue the conversation when I was still so bemused. But I knew this wasn't something that would go away or fix itself. Confusion misted my brain, and the only way for me to see through that and make sense of my own emotions and Davis's intentions was to stop being an avoiding asshole and talk to him.

I just hated the lump that had settled in my gut.

Davis and Libby were my world.

My life.

My eyes connected with Carter when I allowed those thoughts to settle and plant root, reminding me of all I'd fought for over the past couple of years. "Whatever he's thinking, I'll make sure he gets it out of his thick skull and remembers I'm not going anywhere. That I'm happy. Content."

Carter's smile was blinding. "Go buy donuts and arrange a date with that pain-in-the-butt man of yours. Do you want us to have Libby?"

I shook my head. "No, thanks. I need her to be home too, try to have a family dinner where I'm not encouraging her to throw something at her dad's head."

Carter laughed. "You didn't?"

I shrugged. "I didn't stop her when I saw her

holding the broccoli yesterday after reminding us that she hated it."

"You're incorrigible."

"It wasn't aimed at me, and Davis totally deserves it. I'm with Libby. I hate the stuff."

Carter smiled and reminded me about donuts for not only Nicole but for everyone on staff. I huffed out a breath, trying to dispel my bad mood.

Davis and I needed to fix this shit. Seriously, I hadn't had any head for the last couple of nights. Shit was getting real.

I ARRIVED HOME TO LIBBY BUILDING A RACETRACK OUT of blocks for her cars and Davis cooking. From the abrupt silence in the kitchen, I figured he'd heard me come in.

"Hey, Libby. How was school today?" I crouched down on the floor and tugged her on to my lap so I could give her a kiss and a cuddle.

"Good." She giggled when I got to her neck and blew a raspberry.

"You do lots of learning?"

"Yep." She nodded vigorously, and I grinned. She was still a way off being at school, but had made it clear that her daycare was indeed a school where she went to get lots of learning done. Davis and I were all for it, hoping her keenness for learning stayed alive and kicking for as long as possible.

"What's happening here?" I indicated the two cars that were stacked upside down.

"Road wage."

My eyes widened. "Road rage?"

"Yep." She scooted off my lap and pointed at a red monster truck. "She gots mad." Libby gave a dramatic heavy sigh.

"That right? Any reason?" I had no idea where she came up with this stuff.

"They were bad and said no." An adorable pout puffed her bottom lip out.

"Oh, right. Well, saying no isn't always a bad thing."

"Nuh-uh." She shook her head vigorously.

"Dare I ask what they said no about?" Out the corner of my eye, I saw movement to my right. A quick glance over and my gaze fell on Davis, arms folded and leaning against the doorframe. He looked uneasy, his eyes flicking between me and his daughter. His unease punched at my gut. The last two days had been shockingly shit.

Needing to extend an olive branch, I offered a

small smile. He latched on immediately, his shoulders losing some of the tension, his own lips curving upward.

"They said no cookie for dinner." Her eyes were fixed on the monster truck in active avoidance of her dad.

I pressed my lips together to keep from laughing and quirked my brow at Davis. He shrugged and kept quiet.

Looked like I was dealing with this well-thought-out tantrum.

"Cookies are yummy."

She nodded and glanced at me.

"What is it that they have a lot of in them? Do you remember?"

Her nose scrunched, either in thought or disdain, I wasn't sure. "Sugar."

"That's right. And what's always really important before we have a treat like a cookie?"

She tugged up her top, revealing her belly button. "Fill with good stuff and the Cookie Monster can come."

I prodded her tummy and in an atrocious Cookie Monster impression, said, "You want cookie? You need dinner. If not, I'll eat all the cookies."

She threw herself to the floor in hysterics. I took

it as a win. There'd be a day I was sure she'd simply roll her eyes at me. I'd be grateful for every day that didn't happen.

"You silly, Daddy Scott."

I froze. My heart stopped before restarting and going a mile a minute. I couldn't speak. I couldn't see for the emotion filling me up and threatening to spill over.

Holy shit.

Biting hard on my bottom lip, I risked a glance at Davis. Big fucking mistake. The bastard's eyes brimmed with unshed tears, his eyes wide, and if he was anything like me, he wouldn't be able to speak.

I swallowed hard, not wanting to draw attention to her calling me Daddy. All I wanted to do was tug her into my arms and hold her close. So I did just that.

She wriggled around before throwing her arms around my shoulders.

"You 'kay?"

Our ever-perceptive girl was too damn observant for her own good.

"Yeah, baby girl." I managed a nod and gave her a tight squeeze.

She angled away and held my face in the palms of

her small hands. "You sad?" A frown made her brows dip.

"No." I grinned, the action wide and real. "Just very, very happy."

She observed me for another moment before patting me on the head. I laughed and heard Davis sniff.

"I love you, Libby."

"I know." She clambered off my lap. "Loves you back."

Getting myself under control, I glimpsed at Davis. His smile was soft, his emotion high.

"I love you both more," he said. His gaze held mine for a beat, and I felt his words soul deep. "Dinner's ready."

My heart flipped. This... these two people... were mine. While I still had to clear the air with Davis, there was no doubt in my mind that he knew that too.

After two strained evenings, our meal was filled with silliness. Admittedly my emotions were difficult to temper, still reeling from Libby so innocently and naturally claiming me as her own, but my laughter was genuine.

Tension settled between me and Davis, but from words yet to be spoken, not fear of argument.

We were having some downtime, watching a TV show with Libby while coloring.

"Bath's ready, Libby."

She jumped up immediately and made a run for it.

"Tidy up first." Davis's words stopped her in her tracks. Rather than dragging her feet, she raced on back and started dumping her crayons away in her big box. There was no denying Libby loved bath time. After story time, it was her favorite thing to do.

"Dibs on story time tonight," I called out.

"Fine. I get tomorrow."

Davis's wink made my heart speed up. Reassurance danced through me.

After thirty minutes and Davis all but having to drag Libby from the tub, she was dry and tucked up in bed. I lay next to her, book in hand, just finishing off the last page in my best monster voice. "But I didn't want to eat the fairy, even though I was sure she was delicious."

Libby blew out a heavy breath, her eyes wide.

"Were you worried?"

She scrunched up her face. "I think'd he be nice in the end. And Pwetty Petal is such a nice fairy."

I nodded. "She is. She was really kind to the monster."

"Yep." She popped the *P* and followed up with a yawn.

"Come on then. Sleepy time for you. Bathroom first."

Libby held her arms out. "Cawy, pease."

"Sure thing."

I swooped her up and she lay her head on my shoulder, her eyes barely open. After a quick wee stop and wash up, she was back in bed, tucked in, and her night light on.

"You ready for me?" When Davis peered around the slightly open door, I gave him a small nod. "Sweet dreams then." He leaned over and dropped a kiss on her head. "Love you, baby girl."

"Night, night, Dada."

I quirked my brow at that.

"Dada?" Davis smiled down at his daughter. "That's new."

Libby sleepily nodded. "Daddy Scott," she said, as if that explained it all.

Once more, my heart tripped over itself. She'd apparently thought this through.

"I like Dada. Love you."

"Loves you more. To moon." Her eyes were closed.

"Love you, Libby." I dotted a kiss on her head, and she mumbled incoherently under her breath.

We stepped out of her room. Once Libby's door was closed, Davis turned me and backed me up against the wall a few steps away from the door.

"I know we need to clear the air." His breath brushed across my lips, his mouth close as his eyes held mine. "But for the last two days, you've barely let me touch you."

It was true. Too confused for more than a departing kiss in the morning to simply placate, I hadn't been willing to be up close and personal with him, despite my dick being pissed off with me. "I know." It was the only admission I was willing to give.

"That needs to stop." Heat flared in his eyes. From the moment I'd come home, tension had zipped between us, made even more potent after Libby's use of Daddy.

"Okay." Wanting his lips on mine, I was more than happy to comply, to celebrate, to show him how much I loved both him and our girl.

His mouth curved up before he pressed his lips against mine. I expected a bruising kiss, not only because we'd gone without for a couple of days, but because of the finely strung strain between us.

Instead, his lips were supple, warm and inviting. The kiss was delicate, filled with heated promise and love.

His kisses were familiar, welcoming. I eased into the touch, my shoulders relaxing as our lips brushed against each other's. He pulled back, and I exhaled softly, knowing it needed to stop, but hating to let the moment be over.

"Come on." Huskiness filled his voice, making me smile. It was just as difficult to stop for him. He clasped my hand. "Coffee or wine?"

"Wine," I whispered.

With a tug of my hand, he led me away from Libby's room, and we headed to talk this out.

CHAPTER SEVEN

DAVIS

"I wasn't suggesting I was holding you back." Determination threaded through my voice. I needed Scott to hear me. "When I mentioned the town, I literally mean the town, and how small it can be, how narrow-minded some of the people can be. It concerned me, not thinking you're as happy as you could be."

His lips pursed, and I knew he intended to speak, but I needed to finish.

"Let me carry on."

Scott's shoulders loosened and he eased back into the couch a little. "Okay."

I kept my hand on his thigh, wanting the contact between us. Yeah, I was pretty damn sure we should hurry the hell up and move on to the good stuff, but I had zero room for misunderstanding in my life. "What I'm saying is, do you need more?" The crease between Scott's brows appeared immediately. I was quick to add, "The *more* here doesn't mean Libby and I aren't with you every step."

"So what exactly are you suggesting?" His tone was reserved and speckled with unease despite my attempt at reassuring him.

"If you need somewhere bigger, a place with a stronger community who are more accepting, we can move. All of us."

Wide-eyed, he stared back at me, his jaw dropping for a moment before he slammed it shut. "But Libby, your coffee shop... Tanner...." He shook his head. "My sister and the boys...."

My heart constricted. We'd both be giving up a lot if we up and left, but what I'd be gaining in return would be so much more. Scott being at ease and truly happy would make all our lives better. I said as much to Scott.

"And all this because of one drunken night dancing?" His voiced pitched weirdly.

"Well, when you put it like that, no." I shook my head and gave him a wry grin. "I need you to behave the way that's true to you, be at ease with *you*. Not only in your own skin, but with us too." I blew out a heavy breath. "I know Kirkby comes with its own set of miserable history for you." I shrugged, not quite sure how to carry on, especially when he started shaking his head at me, something like bewilderment on his face.

"I think I could punch you."

I snorted. "Excuse me?"

"You, you're a dick." I opened my mouth to speak before he cut me off. "Yes, yes, I know you have a big one." He rolled his eyes at me and continued. "But all of this bullshit since Sunday has been because you were worried I wasn't happy."

"I didn't say that exactly."

He tilted his head back, I was sure cursing me in his head. "No, but you made a mess of telling me you were worried and simply asking me if I was settled and happy. Which I am by the way."

A grimace fell over my face, and I'd never been more relieved that he celebrated that I had a big dick. At this rate, it was the only thing going for me. That and he loved Libby so much. "In my defense, I was hungover and sleep-deprived from shooting my load so much." Both were factually accurate, but were also BS. He knew it as much as I did. I followed up with a wide grin. "But you love me anyway."

Scott angled his head, his gaze scanning my face. My heart flipped when a small smirk appeared on his lips. "I do. So much so, we're staying put."

"Yeah?" I reached for his hand. Comfort at the contact swept through me.

"Yeah. And…."

I waited for a couple of beats, but he kept me hanging. "Are you going to complete the sentence?"

He swallowed thickly, and my curiosity was piqued, especially when he said, "Early spring."

I took the bait and prompted, "What about early spring?"

"Libby will look cute as hell as a flower girl." Pink flushed Scott's cheeks. Meanwhile, my heart raced a mile a minute.

Momentarily speechless and not quite sure if I dared to ask, I gripped his hand tighter, sure my knuckles were white.

Emotion filled his four-word question. "Will you marry me?"

Flip me over and make me scream.

A loud burst of laughter made me jump. Scott's amusement reached his eyes as he said, "Maybe once you've said yes."

I grinned. "I said that aloud, huh?" The break in tension was welcome, helping me get my thoughts together. "Just hold on a second for me." I launched to my feet, leaving Scott on the couch, wide-eyed and open-mouthed.

"You can't be serious!"

"Sorry, I'll be back. Give me a sec." Rushing to our bedroom, my heart threatening to burst free, I almost stumbled over the pile of dirty clothes on the floor, allowing a small smile that Scott hadn't cussed me out. Elation thrummed through me. I was not expecting this now, today. Definitely at some point in the future, and I hoped what I had to give Scott would settle our future for good.

I tugged open the drawer in my bedside table and removed the envelope. Sure that Scott was grumbling like mad and would have been yelling at me for abandoning him if it hadn't been for Libby being fast asleep, I made quick work to return to him.

Mild amusement registered on his face when he saw me, out of breath and a little sweaty. This was huge. This was everything. And I was determined to make it even more perfect.

Once back by his side, I gave him a shit-eating grin. "I love you." My voice hitched, my happiness warring with the emotion snagged in my throat.

Scott eyed the envelope in my hand. "That for me? And that's still not a yes." He didn't look too worried by my stalling, so I took that as a win as I held the envelope out for him.

"This is my question to you, and my answer too." Tears blurred my vision, but I'd be damned if I'd miss a single expression or nuance from the man I loved. No way would I let them spill over. Screw that.

With shaky hands, he took the open envelope from me. He gently tugged out the document while I remembered to breathe. In silence, he scanned it. For seconds that felt like a hell of a lot longer, his eyes roamed and roamed again before finally, they shot up and connected with mine.

"Are you…" A tear fell as he spoke, taking me by surprise. "Are you serious?" He shook his head as his voice caught.

"So fucking sure." I wiped away the wetness and pressed my mouth to his, my own tears spilling. But fuck if I cared at this point. I tasted the salt, our love as I tugged him close and wrapped him in my arms. When I pulled away, I grinned. "Yes."

His smile was wide, and the happiness I'd seen from him a few days ago at the club was nothing compared to the joy radiating off him as he held my heart. "Yes," he said. "I want nothing more than to be Libby's dad."

"Holy shit," I all but freakin' gushed. "Should we wake her and—"

"No," he said with laughter. "We cannot do that." He shook his head and I saw his tears had dried, replaced by wide-eyed happiness. "Nothing has to be rushed."

"But you said spring," I grumbled, not even giving a damn that I sounded needy. I was. I wanted this to happen now, all wrapped up with a dickie bow on top. I snorted at my thoughts.

"What?" Scott's voice lifted in question as he tilted his head. "What's so funny?"

I rolled my eyes at myself. "Just how my brain works sometimes. Just thinking of dickie bows."

Both of Scott's eyebrows launched high. "As in bow ties?"

I nodded and laughed.

"You want us to wear tuxes?"

I snorted at his confusion. I got it. Nothing about me screamed formal and certainly not bow ties. I shrugged. "Not necessarily. I just want you to be mine and us to be a family in every way possible."

The look he gave me, that dreamy-eyed look that he rarely shared, had my heart stuttering with affection. "I think I might geek out or something with wedding plans." Amused horror flashed through me. "Fuck, not sure I'm down with that."

By this point, Scott could no longer contain his amusement at my minor freak-out. His small smiles turned into stomach-hurting laughter, if the way he clutched at his middle was anything to go by. Asshole. "Hey, you laughing at me?"

He couldn't give a straight answer and struggled to get his words out.

"It's not that funny, dick."

"Come here," he barely managed to say, reaching out for me. "You're adorable."

"No, I'm not," I was quick to say, earning me another snort. "I'm a freakin' sex god." I couldn't keep a straight face as I allowed myself to be tugged into his arms. He eased himself on the couch so I was on top of him.

"Sex god, huh?"

I loved the way his body molded with mine, how we fit so well. "Yeah," I said, my voice dropping an octave as it turned husky.

He shifted his hips to brush against my pelvis.

My breath hitched. "Less talking. Details tomorrow."
It was the only warning he gave before he shut me
up with a searing kiss.

———

AROUND BREAKFAST THE NEXT DAY, THE TENSION WAS
thick—but so different from the tension since
returning from our night away. This time, excitement buzzed between us. We'd already decided in
hushed voices during the night that we would definitely aim for spring. Something quiet and local, and
I couldn't wait to tell Libby. The fact that she'd
decided for herself to call Scott Daddy had almost
brought me to my knees the night before.

Any semblance of nerves or worry I may have
had about Scott adopting Libby officially was oblit-
erated at that moment. She'd not only accepted him
into our lives, but she'd made him her own with the
sweetness only a three-year-old could manage.

"Libby," I started, my knee bobbing up and down,
eager to get this off my chest, "yesterday, you know
you called Scott Daddy?"

She paused from playing cars or something that
involved weird *vroom* noises with her half-eaten

toast. Her gaze flicked to Scott, who I saw was smiling broadly at her, and then back to me. "Yes," she answered with a nod. "Is bad?"

"God, no." I was quick to reassure. "You can absolutely call him Daddy."

"I love it, in fact," Scott added, leaning over and dotting a kiss on her head.

She seemed to mull that over a moment before nodding again, and saying, "'Kay." She then went back to her toast.

"Well, baby, we're going to make it official to get proper paperwork that means everyone else will know Scott is your daddy too."

She glanced up at me, remaining quiet.

"Does that sound okay?"

"He aweady my daddy." Confusion colored her words.

"I am, baby girl, but this way it means I'm as much as a daddy to you as Davis, your *daddy* is." Scott frowned at the second use of daddy. "This could kind of get confusing." He grinned.

Libby shook her head. "You Daddy Scott." She then looked at me. "You Dada."

I lifted my brows at the use of the word again. "Okay." I drew the word out while considering something like Papa or Pappy or maybe another alternative—something that sounded badass—would be better, but ended up admitting defeat and saying, "Sounds good to me."

"That mean we all same name?" Her big brown eyes peered up at me and drifted to Scott.

Shit, I had not thought about this. I flicked my gaze to Scott, surprised when he offered me a warm smile.

"Actually, Libby, your… dada"—his lips twitched at that. *Asshole*—"and I are going to get married early next year—"

"Mawied. Like a big, pwetty dwess?" Her eyes lit up with awe. Quickly I pressed my lips together to keep from laughing.

"Well," Scott hedged, "your dada and I won't be wearing a pretty dress as we don't like to wear dresses."

Libby's pout had Scott pausing.

"But you can wear the prettiest dress we can find," he said.

She sat up straighter at that. "'Kay." A quick nod followed before she said, "Why not boys wear dwesses?"

Scott threw me a look, one that screamed "you're it!"

I grinned. "Boys can wear dresses if they want to.

Just like you can wear pants."

Her nose scrunched up. "People meanies to Tommy when he puts pwincess dwess on at school."

My heart ached at her words. "That's not nice at all. No one should be saying mean things ever, especially if someone is just trying to be happy."

Libby nodded long and slow, seeming to contemplate her words. "Marco is a poopyhead. He cwied when I told him to leave Tommy alone and he was a poopyhead."

Scott snorted, drawing my attention to him. He clamped onto his lips, pulling them into his mouth, while my own twitched.

"He does sound like a poopyhead," I admitted. "But if you call him names, it won't make him stop, and you'll end up in trouble. If he's being mean, tell him to leave you alone and get a life."

"Ha! She can't say that," Scott said, laughing.

"Why?" I winked at Libby and grinned at Scott. "It's better than her laying him out." Which was so wrong on so many levels, but screw that. Bullies not squashed at an early age would just get bigger and meaner.

Shaking his head, Scott continued to laugh. "I think what your dada is trying to say, Libby, is yes, tell him to stop and go away. If he doesn't leave, then tell your teacher, and then later us, okay?"

She sighed a little. "'Kay," she reluctantly agreed.

I grinned and continued to drink my coffee while wondering what we were going to do about our names.

CHAPTER EIGHT

SCOTT

"Why did you think a barbecue would be a good idea again?" I rubbed my hands together next to the open flame of the barbecue. Complete in a sweater, coat, and beanie, I arched my brow first at Carter, then at Davis in the distance, uncertain if he could hear me, sure at any moment icicles would be forming.

It was the day before Thanksgiving, and somehow we'd managed to keep our exciting news under wraps for the past week or so. A miracle, since Libby wasn't great at keeping secrets.

Carter's parents were in town for the holiday, and while tomorrow we'd be spending the day with them, we took today as an impromptu engagement party, under the guise of a preholiday get-together.

Ted, Jason, and Davis were currently chatting on the deck while watching Libby, Toby, and Hunter playing ball with Rex. All were racing around, seemingly oblivious to the cold.

Carter grinned at me as he passed his dad, Jack, another beer. "Hey, it wasn't my idea. Don't be blaming me." He flicked his head at Jenna, who was cozied up with Mick at the outside table, while Marcy, Carter's mom, was saying something to make them laugh.

I stared hard at my sister, who I noted was holding hands with Mick. As though feeling my gaze on her, she looked in my direction and stuck her tongue out at me when I raised my brows.

"Real mature," I called out. She returned a none-too-subtle middle finger at me across her cheek.

Their date had apparently gone well. And while I still hadn't had the overbearing-big-brother chat with Mick yet, Jenna wasn't a lovesick teenager. She knew what she was doing, and from what I knew about Mick, I had to agree with Davis when he'd said he was a good guy.

"Your sister seems happy," Jack said, sounding amused at our exchange.

I looked at the older man and gave him a nod. "Yeah, she is. The boys really like Mick too."

Jenna had been worried about introducing Hunter and Toby to Mick, which I knew Davis could relate to, thinking back to my first time meeting Libby. But she needn't have worried. The boys thought he was amazing. He was already supporting Jenna and them, and from what I could see, was doing a hell of a lot more than Jenna's dick of an ex had ever done.

"That's good," Jack responded. "Joining a ready-made family I imagine can be difficult."

"And all kinds of wonderful," I said with a smile, taking a moment to watch Libby chase Hunter around the garden.

"I keep telling our boy here that it's about time he grew his family." Jack threw a pointed look at Carter, who rolled his eyes at his dad.

"It's happening. We're in full puppy mode." A soft smile appeared on Carter's face. "And I think we've finally found the perfect girl for us. Let me show you a picture." He tugged out his phone to show us a photo of a beautiful Rhodesian. "She's only fifteen weeks. Can you believe people have given her up? We're going to the Rhodesian rescue place as soon as they reopen after the holidays." He practically buzzed with excitement.

"Puppy grandkids." Jack put an arm around his

son and squeezed. "Sounds good to me. She's a pretty girl."

"Isn't she!" Carter gushed. "It'll be so good for Rex to have someone to look after and play with too."

"I think you'll find she'll soon rule the roost," Lauren added as she joined us.

Carter laughed. "I have no doubt you're right." He tucked his phone away. "Anything else need doing?" he asked me, eyeing the cooking food.

"Unless you can turn the temperature up a bit so it's not freeze-your-balls-off cold, I think I'm good, thanks." Carter snorted in amusement as I continued. "The steaks are done. We should be about ready to eat."

"Did someone say something about balls?" Jasper said as he entered through the back gate. "I'm pretty good at juggling them." He bobbed his eyebrows up and down, causing a groan from the majority of us. "Sorry I'm late." He indicated over his shoulder. "I hope it's okay I brought a plus one."

I glanced behind him, my eyes widening in surprise. "Ian?"

"Hey." He gave an awkward wave. "I hope it's okay I'm here. I brought cocktail mix and pie."

"Good to see you, Ian." Davis stepped into my line of sight and shook his hand before taking the pie off him. "You're more than welcome." He cast a gaze at me, eyebrows high. I gave him a smile and small shrug. Davis hadn't said anything about Ian and Jasper keeping in touch, not that him being here was an issue. Just a surprise. "I'll get this in the kitchen for later," Davis said.

He turned and headed inside as Jasper stepped toward us, Ian in tow.

After a quick introduction, I announced the steak was ready.

Davis rounded up the kids, and we spread out on the chairs and tables we'd put up, all vying for the sunshine spilling into the yard that we hoped would help to take off the chill. Thank Christ we'd done this during the daytime rather than tonight.

"So, is this young man your beau?" Marcy asked as soon as there was a lull while we ate. "I've never seen or heard of you before, Ian. Jasper, have you been hiding him from us?"

I coughed a little, my food threatening to travel the wrong way.

Jasper laughed good-naturedly. "No, Mrs. Falon. Ian and I are friends. We've only recently met."

Marcy's gaze zeroed in on Ian, who looked a little uncomfortable under her scrutiny. I understood it. Marcy was a force of nature.

"Mom," Carter said, "every man here doesn't need to be attached. Leave them be." He sent Ian an apologetic smile.

"I wasn't saying they had to. I was just curious. How do you all know each other?" Marcy took a sip of her wine after she spoke.

"We met not long ago at a club. The same time I met Davis and Scott," Ian said, his tone friendly.

"Ooh…" Marcy leaned in a little. "What sort of club?" She looked over at the kids, I assumed to see if they were listening in, which did not bode well for Ian. "Did it have holes in the wall?"

"Mom!"

I choked on my beer. Bubbles flew out of my nose, and I hacked loudly. Davis's hand quickly pounded on my back while his shoulder jiggled from laughter.

"Seriously, Mom, you can't say or ask stuff like that." Poor Carter looked horrified, while Ian's cheeks flamed. Wide-eyed, he appeared to not know what the hell to do. I got it. I really did. And I had to admit, I was relieved as hell not to be on the end of her random questioning.

"Erm, no, Mrs. Falon," Jasper answered, amusement lifting his words. "As intriguing as that sounds, it was just a regular old club."

Marcy seemed to deflate a little. "That's a little disappointing. I've always wanted to go to one of those clubs."

"Oh my God, Mom, for the love of all that is holy, please stop. Dad." Carter stared at his dad in horror.

"No good asking me to rein her in, son. It's best she gets these questions off her chest. If not, she'll only start googling." Jack shuddered.

"So, Tanner," Carter said quickly, "did you tell everyone about that new project you started?"

Davis snorted beside me, and I looked at Tanner, who stared at his boyfriend in obvious confusion.

"Actually, we have some news." Davis, ever the lifesaver, stood up, pulling everyone's attention to him. He glanced down at me and winked. I grinned up at him, more than happy for our news to be out there, especially if it helped save poor Ian and Jasper. "Two things, actually." Holding out his hand for me to take, he continued as I stood and gripped it. "We're turning today's preholiday festivities into an engagement party."

When my sister gasped, my eyes immediately found hers. Her hand covered her mouth while her eyes filled with tears. I swallowed at the unexpected emotion.

"This gorgeous doctor"—I rolled my eyes, making our friends and family laugh—"of mine asked me to marry him."

A squeal came from Ted, and Jason clamped an arm down on him.

"Next spring, we'll be getting married in Kirkby, and want you all to celebrate with us."

Jenna bounced out of her seat just as Davis pulled me in for a tender kiss. A moment later, Jenna launched herself at us and tugged us both into a hug.

"I am so happy for you both." Tears slipped over her cheeks. "Oh my God, like so happy." She squeezed again, and I leaned down and planted a kiss on her head.

As Tanner patted Davis on the back and everyone came closer to give their congratulations, my hearing zeroed in on "Daddy Scott, why Aunty Jenna cwying?"

I scooted down to her level as Jenna did another gasp and moved out of Libby's way. "She's just very happy that we're getting married," I said, scooping her up.

Libby nodded and then peered over at my sister. "We is all getting mawied and I is making Daddy

Scott my weal daddy," she announced proudly. "And I is getting a pwetty dwess."

Tanner's voice reached me. "Adoption?"

I watched Davis nod while grinning widely. "Yep."

Tanner's eyes connected with mine. So much had happened since the first time we'd met, when he'd hated me. My heart picking up speed took me by surprise. Tanner was the closest thing to family Davis had outside of me and Libby. His approval would matter to Davis. It mattered to me.

He bobbed his head and smiled. "About time. That's great news," Tanner said, wrapping Davis up in a hug.

I exhaled and planted a kiss on Libby's cheek, who had since grown bored and was asking to be put down.

"We need champagne!" Ted called out amongst the laughter and happy conversation.

I squeezed Davis's hand as I said, "There's some in the fridge in the shed."

Davis turned to me. "There is?" His brows lifted in surprise. "When did you do that?"

I shrugged and planted another kiss on his soft lips. "Yesterday."

"I love you," he mumbled against my mouth.

"I know," I said, pulling away. "Love you too, baby."

In the time it took for me to pull my gaze from Davis and check that Libby hadn't snuck off to play and was still eating, Jason appeared, carrying four bottles of champagne, while his husband walked at his side, no doubt ready to take over and pop the corks.

"You know," Ted said, his gaze pointedly on Davis, "mine and Jason's wedding anniversary is March 15, it could be a perfect time—"

"No," Davis said quickly, shaking his head. "You're incorrigible."

"Two birds—"

Jason cut Ted off. "Ted, I don't think Davis and Scott want to double up their wedding with our anniversary."

I swore Jason had a special gift. He seemed the only guy able to wrangle Ted. I glanced at Marcy, then at Carter, who met my eyes wearing a similar grin. I laughed, wondering whether he'd have the same ability on Marcy.

"It was just a suggestion," Ted said, a little subdued, "but"—*maybe not*—"I was thinking a circus theme. Think clowns and juggling and—"

"I can totally juggle balls! I wasn't lying earlier," Jasper piped up, and Davis and Jason groaned in unison.

"No," I practically shouted, thinking back to Libby's first birthday party with a shudder.

"I'll help cater, but for the love of God, no extra balls," Davis pleaded.

I snorted and received a squeeze on my ass for doing so. "Ouch," I said, laughing.

"Don't encourage him, else I'll make the clowns happen," Davis whispered. His gaze connected with mine.

"You wouldn't."

He arched a brow in challenge.

As I listened to the developing crazy discussion of circuses, nightmare clowns, and anniversary and wedding celebrations, I placed my hand in Davis's back pocket and stood close.

This felt like more than simply the start of our lives together, of truly becoming us. This life we'd created for ourselves—arguments, misunderstandings, and crazy friends and family, was everything.

And I wouldn't change a single thing.

. . .

THE END

Be on the lookout for Jasper's story, a full-length novel.

THANKS

THANKS FOR READING *BECOMING US*. I DO HOPE YOU enjoyed Davis and Scott's follow-up story. I appreciate your help in spreading the word, including telling a friend. Before you go, it would mean so much to me if you would take a few minutes to write a review and share how you feel about my story so others may find my work. Reviews really do help readers find books. Please leave a review on your favorite book site.

ACKNOWLEDGMENTS

You're all rock stars! Thank you for coming back and wanting more.

ABOUT THE AUTHOR

Becca Seymour lives and breathes all things book related. Usually with at least three books being read and two WiPs being written at the same time, life is merrily hectic. She tends to do nothing by halves, so happily seeks the craziness and busyness life offers.

Living on her small property in Queensland with her human family as well as her animal family of cows, chooks, and dogs, Becca appreciates the beauty of the world around her and is a believer that love truly is love.

To check for updates head to Becca's website:
https://beccaseymour.com
You can sign up for her newsletter here:
https://mailchi.mp/4d9f2a5109b8/becca-seymour
Plus, join her Facebook group, which she shares with the awesome Louisa Masters here:
https://www.facebook.com/
groups/seymourbookswithmasterfulmen/

ALSO BY BECCA SEYMOUR

Coming Home Collection

Realigned (FREE)

Amalgamated

Remedied (Coming 2020)

True-Blue Series

Let Me Show You (#1)

I've Got You (#2)

Becoming Us (#3)

Stand-Alone MM Urban Fantasy Romance

Thicker Than Water

SNEAK PEEK

THICKER THAN WATER (AN URBAN FANTASY ROMANCE) BY BECCA SEYMOUR

Love shifters? Love urban fantasy romance? And most of all, love the characters' voices and worlds I create? Then, everything crossed, you're going to love *Thicker Than Water*.

CHAPTER ONE EXCERPT

Heat rippled over my skin. The singed scent of hair clogged my ability to scent the way out, leaving me momentarily cursing my stubbornness for going this alone. My boss would never let me live it down if I got myself charred to a crisp or killed. At least the latter would mean I wouldn't have to listen to his pompous spiel about following protocol. The dick had it out for me. He had since I'd joined the team three years ago, and despite my success rate on missions, he hadn't taken kindly to the son of the Blackheath alpha joining the Supernatural Investigation & Crime Bureau.

Creaking beams followed by the crash of timber had me blinking hard against the blackening smoke. There had to be a way out. While Brent, my division leader, thought I was foolhardy—or perhaps simply a fool—I had studied the schematics of the lab prior to entering. What I hadn't planned for was Jonas Cartwright to set the damn thing on fire with me in it.

Focussed on pushing my senses beyond the sound of the licking fire and groaning foundations, I closed my eyes, hoping for a ripple, something, anything that would get me out of this situation. Two beats, three, four... but nothing. I could either stay planted, hoping a miracle would happen, or I could act. Neither seemed like a smart move but staying put and being roasted was not an option. The raw heat travelling up my arms, removing my hairs along the way, cried out for my retreat.

Action it was.

In barely a split second, my eyes shifted. While the heightened sight wouldn't help with the smoke, the electricity had been tripped by the fire, and I needed all the help I could get.

I cursed up a storm in my head as I raced the way I'd come. With a leap over a toppled cabinet, a swerve away from the licks of fire trailing along workstation dividers, I swore the whole time I would find Cartwright and put him to ground once and for all. The way ahead was blocked, and no barrelling through would solve that. I screeched to a stop. "Shit." I looked left and right, thinking hard about the drawings I'd glanced at ten seconds before entering the lab. Screw Brent and his demands for being well-prepared. I had no doubt my name, Callen, was already a regular curse from him. This would simply give him more ammunition. It was better than him seething my surname Blackheath I supposed, but still, ten seconds of my eyes roaming over the layout was as good as studying in my world.

Before I could figure out my next move, a small scrape of metal to my left had me turning in that direction. I seriously hoped I wasn't racing towards more flames, but the sound was distinctive, controlled.

On reaching a hallway I didn't recognise, I stumbled. "What the hell?" At the end of the darkened hallway was a glass door. While smoke spiralled through the space, it wasn't as black, the fire not yet having reached the area. I crouched low to avoid the white smoke, my eyes focussed on the hand scratching against the glass door. Blood smeared with every gentle swipe of the hand, the movement slowing down.

No one was supposed to be here. Ignoring the fact that Cartwright had blown my half-arsed recon out of the window and taken me by surprise, there seriously shouldn't have been anyone else on site. An unfamiliar edge of panic flared to life in my chest. This was not good.

I charged towards the glass, stopping short of barrelling into it to try the handle. It wouldn't have been the first time I'd broken down a door unnecessarily. I didn't want to crash through a glass door unless I had to. While I healed quickly, shards of glass cutting through my skin still hurt something rotten.

Testing the handle with one hand, I hit the glass lower down, trying to get the attention of the person attempting to get out. Their bloody hand twitched at the loud thud. "Shit," I grumbled. The door was locked. "Hey." I beat against the glass panel harder. It was partially misted for privacy, and visibility was unclear. Unable to tell who was on the other side or whether the smoke had breached the room from another direction, for once, I considered my options.

"Hey." I tried again, my hand smacking the glass harder, not yet intending to break through. "Can you hear me?" Steadying my breath took concentration, but I needed to listen carefully.

"Code." The voice was gravelly. "P-Panel."

I searched quickly and found a panel off to my right. "I need the code." Each word came out calm and clear. Panicking now could possibly get us both killed.

"Five." A cough wracked through him, loud and sounding painful. I squinted, wondering what the hell this guy had been through. "Two. Seven. Seven. Four. Nine."

I hit the numbers as he said them.

"Hash," he finished, and the door clicked, swinging open when the guy fell against it. He landed on the floor.

Unconscious at my feet, the man was sprawled on his front. I tugged him to the side. With no idea where we were, I couldn't simply throw the guy over my shoulder and start racing around, hitting dead ends and burning doors wherever we went. Decision made, I cast a quick glance at the man. Wet blood covered his rich black skin, but his moving chest indicated he was breathing. Barely. Christ, I hoped he didn't die on me. After a final glance, I rushed into the unlocked room. Just because it had been sealed from the inside didn't mean I wouldn't be able to get through another exit.

A door on the opposite side of the room was my target. I headed straight there, spotting vials and another room off to my right. Before I reached the exit, the scent hit me. Blood, and it wasn't from the unconscious lab tech in the hallway. I took a tentative step in the direction the scent came from, bile already churning in my gut.

No. It couldn't be.

Another step forward and I held my breath, not wanting to believe it could be true.

Wide-eyed, I gasped for breath, then regretted the action immediately. Metallic, familiar, and dead. The combination of the three threatened to buckle my knees. Unable to look away, I stared hard, hating every second. But I had to do this. Flesh, torn muscle, mutilated claws; the image seared itself into my mind. Once there, a shockwave of pain ripped through me.

No.

This time I let my knees go and landed on the

floor, my knee finding the blood the same shade of my own. It was her. Hazel. My baby sister.

Find out what happens in *Thicker Than Water*.

The above excerpt is subject to further changes and revisions.

CPSIA information can be obtained
at www.ICGtesting.com
Printed in the USA
BVHW042243210522
637733BV00006B/115